Encyclopedia Horrifica

The Terrifying TRUTH! About Vampires, Ghosts, Monsters, and More

Joshua Gee

Scholastic Inc.

New York   Toronto   London   Auckland   Sydney
Mexico City   New Delhi   Hong Kong   Buenos Aires

Library of Congress Cataloging-in-Publication data is available.

ISBN 13: 978-0-439-92255-5
ISBN 10: 0-439-92255-0

Book Design by Tim Hall, Kay Petronio, and Joshua Gee
Cover Design by Tim Hall
Endpapers by Joshua Gee

12 11 10 9 8 7 6 5 4 3   8 9 10 11 12/0

Printed in Hong Kong
First printing, August 2007

TURN BACK! NOW! WHILE YOU STILL CAN!

Yes, it's a suggestion I hear almost every day. Obviously, I am deaf to those words. Turning back is never really an option for a person in my line of work. Wherever curiosity leads me, I have no choice but to follow.

What is my work, exactly? Well, the time has come to tell you.

Ever since I was a child—small and sickly but cunning nonetheless—my quest has been to unmask the origins of fright. From the day I was old enough to read, I plagued Mother Gee with one bold query after another:

> *Did Dracula ever exist?*
>> *Is there life on other planets?*
>>> *Are some houses truly haunted?*

Most of the time, Mother refused to answer. She was too busy shielding me from sunlight, dust mites, and other airborne dangers. But not always...

On one occasion, she handed me a strange book. I'd never seen it in our house before. It contained startling facts about the Kraken, that hideous armful lurking in many a seaman's nightmares. Much to my delight, the author declared that the Kraken was based on an actual creature. A real-life monster!

"If my favorite thirty-foot cephalopod is real," I wheezed excitedly, "then tell me...what other surprises prowl this planet and beyond?"

Silence was Mother's reply. She hadn't meant to tutor me in terror. No, her mission was to protect me. As the next sixteen chapters will prove to you, my own mission became something very different.

Not everyone is destined for such a quest. That's why we have a special policy here at headquarters. The rules require us to say one thing to unsuspecting ~~victims~~ visitors. Just this once, I must offer to you those same seven words that I am so unwilling to obey:

Turn back. Now. While you still can.

In truth, the decision belongs only to you....

— JG

JOSHUA GEE
Chief Investigator of the Unexplained
ENCYCLOPEDIA HORRIFICA

Contents

TURN BACK! NOW! WHILE YOU STILL CAN! A Welcome Letter from Investigator Gee **iii**

MEMORANDUM FROM HORRIFIC HEADQUARTERS **vi**

PART ONE: Real Nightmares 1

DRACULA LIVES! 2
Meet Dracula(s) | Monster Mash: Hollywood's Dracula vs. History's Dracula | On Being a Vampire Hunter | On Being a Vampire | Special Investigation: E.H. Examines the True Origins of the Most Famous Vampire Ever | Mother Stoker's Spooky Stories | *Dracula*'s Secret Ending | Bat Facts | The 1800s: Vampires Make Headlines | *Nosferatu* | Vampire Killing Kits

IT CAME FROM THE SEA! 10
What Are Globsters? | A Kraken Attackin'! | Trackin' the Kraken: Rare Evidence of the Giant Squid | How Giant Is Giant? | The Terrifying TOOTH: Watch Out for Sharks | Ghost Ship: The *Flying Dutchman* | Ghost Photo: The S.S. *Watertown* | Special Investigation: E.H. Learns the True Story of a Famous Fake | Meet the Feejee Mermaid | Christopher Columbus & Historical Mer-Sightings

ALIEN INVASION! 20
Ufology | Close Encounter of the First Kind [CEI]: Alleged UFO Photos | A Time Line of Alien Life on Earth | CE2: The Mystery of the Fused Sand | Crop Circles | Top-Secret Satellite Image of Area 51 in Nevada | CE3: The Most Famous UFO Ever | CE4: Abducted by the Light | Alien Spacecraft or Swamp Gas? | The Alien Cemetery Hoax | CE5: The (Very) Long-Distance Call | CE6: An Alien Death-Ray? | CE7: The Most Horrific Close Encounter of All

HOWLING AT THE MOON! 28
A Human's Guide to Werewolves | A Werewolf's Guide to Werewolves | The Beast of Gévaudan: Was It a Werewolf? | Famous French Werewolves | Monster Mash: Hollywood's Werewolf vs. History's Werewolf | Cloning the Tasmanian Wolf | Does the Moon Affect Behavior? | Is This a Painting of a Werewolf? | Half Man, All Horrible

PART TWO: "That's the Spirit!" 35

BEWARE OF GHOSTS! 36
Meet Bloody Mary | *Tsukumogami*: Artifact Spirits | Haunted Vehicles | The Bell Witch Today | John Bell: Murdered by a Ghost? | House on the Hudson | "As a Matter of Law, the House Is Haunted." | Gift-Giving Ghosts? | Q & A with Loyd "Professor Paranormal" Auerbach | The Three Kinds of Ghosts | Ghost Story: The Haunted

TO CATCH A GHOST! 46
How to Catch a Ghost | *Ghostbusters* (1975/1984) | Thomas Edison: Ghost Hunter? | Ghost-Hunting Gear: Then | Ghost-Hunting Gear: Now | Special Investigation: Can E.H. Survive the Night in a Haunted House? | The Eight Stages of a Ghost Hunt | Ghost Story: His Name Is George | Electronic Voice Phenomena (EVP)

PHANTOMS ON FILM! 58
The Most Famous Ghost Photo of the Twentieth Century: Read a Long-Lost Eyewitness Account | Meet the Brown Lady of Raynham Hall | Why Do Ghosts Wear Clothes? | Early Photographic Frauds | How to View a Ghost Photo | Six Photos: Can You Tell a Ghost from a Hoax?

PERMANENT PETS! 66
Ghost Story: The Invisible Cat | Are These Photos of Ghost Cats? | History's Spookiest Cats | Man's Best Fiend: Dogs Can Be Spooky, Too | Ghost Story: The Phantom Ferret of Middle Village | Pet Cemeteries | "Pet Sematary," by the Ramones | The Cluck Stops Here

PART THREE: Every Day Is Halloween 71

ODD SHOPS & EERIE EATERIES! 72
E.H. Gears Up for a Mission | Come Geocaching in N.Y.C. | Three Frightful Places to Feed | Skulls, Bugs, & Other Shopping Needs | Meet the Puppet-Master

AMAZING BRAIN WAVES! 80
Photographic Evidence of Telekinesis? | Special Investigation: E.H. Uncovers the Truth About a Top-Secret Government Research Program | Q & A with Psychic Spy Paul H. Smith | What is the Matrix? | Miscellaneous Secret Documents to Enjoy | "My Dad Was a Psychic Spy!" | The Sony Psychic-Station? | Test Yourself for ESP

THE BLACK CAT'S PATH! 90
Fearology | Meet the Bogeymen | 233 Phobias | True Superstitions: Four Believers | Tough Luck: An Experiment in Fear

THE FORBIDDEN BOOKSHELF! 100
Most Horrific Books: "And the Winners Are..." | Special Investigation: E.H. Finds Out If an Evil Book Described by H. P. Lovecraft Was Actually Real | Meet the Cthulhu Monster | The Ancient Egyptian "Book of the Dead" | Uncover *FATE* Magazine

PART FOUR: Fearsome Fates 105

TO BE OR NOT ZOMBIE! 106
Zombie Schoolgirls Attack! | Eight Things You Need to Know About Zombies | The *Zombi* Fate of Clairvius Narcisse | How to Speak *Zombi* | Wade (*The Serpent and the Rainbow*) Davis and the Recipe for "*Zombi* Poison"

TRICKED BY PIXIES! 112
Which One Is a Faerie? | Fooled by Mother Nature: Ugly Trees & "Fairy Rings" | A Famous Author Finds Faeries | Cottingley Photo #5: Can YOU Find Faeries? | The Top Five Most Horrific Hoaxes | Photographic Evidence of the World's Tiniest Terrors

THE CURSE OF THE MUMMY! 118
The Alleged Curse of King Tut | Genuine Threats Faced by Real-Life "Tomb Raiders" | Postcards from Cursed Places | A 45.52-Carat Curse? | The *Sports Illustrated* Cover Jinx & Other Sports Curses | Special Investigation: E.H. Ventures into a Forest That Is Said to Be Cursed

GRUESOME GOOD-BYES! 124
A Biography of Death | Can You Find Death in This Picture? | Meet the Grim Reaper | Death Gets the Last Laugh | The Innocent Woman Who Committed (Miniature) Murder | Dollhouse Murder(?!?) Scene: The Chief Is Missing!

SELECTED BIBLIOGRAPHY 130

INDEX 133

PICTURE CREDITS 136

ROSTER 138

Memorandum from Horrific Headquarters

—————————————————————————— USA

To: **Our Fellow Fear Seekers**
From: **H.Q.**
Re: **How to Experience This Book**

Submitted for your approval: A nonfiction compendium of all things ghoulish and ghastly. The facts and photos contained herein have been carefully investigated, fear-tested, and quality-approved so that only the most terrifying evidence made the cut—and not a sliver less.

Although many experts and eyewitnesses were interviewed for this book, ENCYCLOPEDIA HORRIFICA does not always provide <u>all</u> possible scientific or historical answers to each question. (If it did, the only word on the cover would be ENCYCLOPEDIA!) Nonetheless, we can assure you that we steadfastly pursue all of the most slithery, undead, repulsive, and/or foul-smelling answers to each question.

As you join us on this merriest of quests, please beware of ghosts and wear your regulation Paranormal Investigator Hat at all times. If you master the fear facts, we might even recruit you. After all, one can never predict when Investigator Gee might unexpectedly... *retire.*

HORRIFIC HYPERJUMP

Gotta fly? Here's a handy guide to but a few of the unpleasant pictures ahead.

WITNESS THE MOST HORRIFIC	TURN TO PAGE
Vampire	9
Sea Monster, Unreal	11
Sea Monster, Real	12
Tentacles	13
Feejee Mermaids	18
Alien	25
Witness, Scared Witless	53
Ghost Photo	58
"Ectoplasm"	61
Headquarters	73
"Mitten-Biters"	90
Eyeballs	100
Cthulhu Monster	103
Zombie Schoolgirls	106
Optical Illusion #1	113
Pickled Dragon	116
Micro-Monsters	117
Optical Illusion #2	124

Part One

Do you like scary movies? We do. Screaming keeps the lungs healthy and fit.

But how do you feel about scary movies that are true?

If you can't think of any, you're in for a shocking surprise. Some of Hollywood's greatest horrors are lurking in the scariest of places—the real world.

Prepare to find out once and for all if a werewolf's bark is worse than its bite, plus the answers to many other crucial questions.

Movie fans, look beneath your beds for...

Real Nightmares

DRACULA LIVES!

MEET THE ROMANIAN RULER BEHIND BRAM STOKER'S BLOODSUCKER.

Perhaps you've already met Count Dracula—that cape-twirling star of movies, TV shows, and video games. Perhaps you've even read 1897's *Dracula*, by Bram Stoker. He was the author who first combined fact and fantasy to create a Romanian nobleman with a thirst for blood.

But have you ever met the *actual* Dracula?

Five centuries ago, one Romanian nobleman did indeed prey upon the weak. Although he was never believed to be a vampire, he blazed a murderous trail of blood that partly inspired Stoker's book. The man's name? Prince Vlad III of Wallachia—better known as Vlad Dracula.

Travel to modern-day Wallachia, Romania, and you will discover many tourist attractions—Dracula's Palace, Castle Dracula, even the Dracula Club Restaurant. At these places, you may wear your favorite plastic fangs any time you please.

But if it's true horror you crave? Proceed to nearby Snagov Lake as the sun begins to set . . . and pay no attention to the howling of Romania's wild wolves.

Soon you will spot an island. As you peer into the fog, you might hear somebody cry, "Nu intră!" ("Do not go there!"). For upon that island lies the tomb of Vlad Dracula—*terror* in any language.

The most unsettling fact about Dracula's tomb is not its owner's name. Far scarier is what archaeologists discovered there. In the prince's most likely burial spot they found . . . nobody at all. When they finally dug up some princely remains nearby, those oddly vanished, too.

Could it be because Vlad Dracula still needs his body today? Some locals believe the answer is a bloodcurdling **yes!**

Sword-wielding statue of Vlad Dracula in Romania, where *Drăculea* means "devil."

Dracula's tomb, 1938: Did he step out to get a bite to eat?

32 USA

Bela Lugosi as *DRACULA*

MONSTER MASH

Who would win in a furious fight to the (un)death? YOU decide.

HOLLYWOOD'S DRACULA	VERSUS	HISTORY'S DRACULA
Eighty years old. The definitive *Dracula* starred Bela Lugosi and debuted in 1931.	AGE	Five centuries old. The reputation of Vlad Dracula (1431–1476) never dies.
Maybe. It's his current mailing address.	BORN IN TRANSYLVANIA?	Probably. Historians believe Vlad's birthplace was real-life Transylvania, Romania.
Prefers the comfort of his own coffin	FAVORITE HANGOUTS	Preferred luxurious Targoviste Palace, south of Transylvania
Four*	NUMBER OF VICTIMS	Tens of thousands
Sharp teeth	FAVORITE WEAPONS	Six-foot wooden spears
Black cape, tuxedo, and pretty amulet	FASHION STATEMENT	Crowns, helmets, and impenetrable armor
Count	TITLE	*Voivode*, or "Warrior Prince"
Yes	CAN HE FLY?	No
No	CAN HE FIGHT?	Yes
Allergic to garlic, sunlight, and wooden stakes	WEAKNESSES	Although he ruled with an iron fist, Vlad was all thumbs when it came to politics and peacekeeping.
Abraham Van Helsing, professor and vampire hunter	ENEMIES	Hungary, Turkey, and even Vlad's own brother, Radu the Handsome

*Average number of victims in six popular Dracula films (total onscreen victims per film, divided by six): 1922's *Nosferatu*, 1931's *Dracula*, 1958's *Horror of Dracula*, 1977's *Count Dracula*, 1992's *Bram Stoker's Dracula*, and 2004's *Van Helsing*.

ON BEING A VAMPIRE HUNTER

Central European tradition is very specific when it comes to identifying a vampire's grave.

Step #1: Obtain a young male horse. Its hide must be as black as the blackest ocean.

Step #2: Guide the horse through the graveyard. Over one grave the horse shall refuse to pass.

Step #3: Summon additional villagers for backup. You're going to need all the help you can get.

Step #4: Begin digging. . . .

Above all else, remember that daylight suits your mission best, as the vampire may be making housecalls by moonlight.

DID YOU KNOW that Buffy Summers, better known as TV's *Buffy the Vampire Slayer*, might have been named after Montague Summers? An expert monster chaser, he wrote such helpful texts as *The Vampire: His Kith and Kin* (1928).

HIGH STAKES

When defending yourself against the undead, your garlic, crosses, and holy water won't always last the night. Your secret weapon is a wooden stake—simple, elegant, and deadly. ENCYCLOPEDIA HORRIFICA endorses stakes made from white thorn (*Acacia constricta*), a small tree that requires much sunlight. If you live in the American southwest, you've probably seen it growing wild. If you don't live there, go there. Now! Sometimes the correct type of wood is all that stands between vampire and victim.

ON BEING A VAMPIRE

Whether you're a Bulgarian *ubour* or a West Indian *loogaroo*, you are never alone. Vampire folklore has existed around the globe for many centuries. The earliest known vampire is depicted in Babylonian artwork that's 2,300 years old! Sadly, you probably won't bump into that vampire today! Even in that ancient image, the poor, defenseless bloodsucker was being threatened by a mean, old vampire hunter with a stake.

"VAMPIRES RULE!"

Sure, anybody can tell you that. But have you ever noticed that vampires obey a lot of rules, too? In fact, bloodsuckers of all ages must follow more rules than most ghosts, reanimated corpses, and mummies combined. Here are a few examples:

- Never play outside after sunrise.
- No yummy Italian dishes—too much garlic.
- Hide your fangs from humans—except during meals.
- Ask a friend to comb your hair. (Mirrors won't work!)

In the market for a new coffin? Always buy, never rent. Although it may not look like much, it's home-sweet-home . . . forever. It will protect you from death-by-sunburn and conceal you from vampire hunters. You do have options: Count Dracula never travels without a coffin full of native Romanian soil, while Polish vampires traditionally suggest that you fill up your home-sweet-home with blood-sweet-blood.

EH SPECIAL INVESTIGATION

PHILADELPHIA, PENNSYLVANIA—"This is the 'coffin,'" says Dracula expert Michael Barsanti as he unclasps a faded gray box. It's much too small to be an actual coffin, yet its contents are just as bone-chilling.

Mr. Barsanti slowly withdraws numerous see-through plastic envelopes. Most of them contain a one-of-a-kind note (pictured) handwritten by the author of *Dracula*; all of them are over a century old. Imagine the notes you might jot down while researching a history paper—if the class were all about the history of vampires and werewolves.

As Mr. Barsanti turns from one yellowing page to the next, an eerie thought sets in: *Bram Stoker based his novel on people's actual sightings.* Obsessed with telling the most realistic tale possible, Stoker lingered all night in gaslit libraries, hunting for the ghoulish folklore he needed to fuel his imagination. For more than half a decade, he studied countless books and newspapers, taking notes on only the most persuasive evidence he could find.

If we could ask Stoker himself whether or not he believed in vampires and werewolves, what might he say? Well, hopefully nothing. After all, he's been dead since 1912!

Michael Barsanti at the Rosenbach, site of the Dracula Festival every October.

A MEDIEVAL MANUSCRIPT. A TROUBLING TRUTH.

The Rosenbach also possesses a rare text about fifteenth-century ruler Vlad Dracula. It might have been written by an eyewitness to his fiendish deeds.

Called "Dracole Waida" and published in Germany in 1488, the pamphlet is said to be one of only seven in the entire world. Its kindly keepers invited ENCYCLOPEDIA HORRIFICA to examine the priceless item, which must rank among the first printed horror stories ever.

Naturally, we took that as a dare. A silly old relic? Written by amateurs? How horrific could it truly be?

Oh, but we were wrong to snicker. Dead wrong.

To open up the volume and sit alone with it—alongside an English translation—is to discover the *real* reasons why Vlad Dracula eventually became known as *Vlad Țepeș*, or "Vlad the Impaler." Impalement was a medieval form of torture and murder. It's best described in a foreign language that the reader does not understand, best confined to a tiny volume tucked away in an obscure library, and best ignored by

This 1488 portrait of Vlad Dracula bleeds with color, as if painted yesterday.

ENCYCLOPEDIA HORRIFICA forevermore.

But before that, just . . . one . . . more . . . page . . .

A pretty grisly page: It reads that Vlad's victims accumulated on his front lawn like "a mighty forest"! EH

"Certainly till I was about seven years old I never knew what it was to stand upright."

Those were the words of *Dracula*'s creator. He was always sick for reasons nobody knows to this day. In the 1850s, there was no television—or even electricity—but Stoker still had entertainment. His mother was an expert on spooky Irish folklore, which may explain why he loved to frighten people as an adult. Her tales of scary mischief makers must have seemed pretty real to a boy who never left the house.

PHOOKAS Much like werewolves, these faerie folk can turn into dogs, horses, or bulls. They sometimes offer rides to weary travelers. Don't accept!

BANSHEES Listen carefully. You may hear these ghastly hags wailing in the wind. Their sorrowful song always predicts the death of a loved one.

MERROWS To defeat one of these scaly sea creatures, steal its red feathered cap. It will swim no more.

DRACULA II: THE SEQUEL?

Days before *Dracula* was published in 1897, Bram Stoker made a sudden last-minute change to the story. In the original version, the author had described the complete destruction of Dracula's castle—and with it, Dracula's future! Some experts believe Stoker ended up leaving the castle intact because he planned to write a sequel someday. Stoker's intentions are still a mystery, though.

ENCYCLOPEDIA HORRIFICA is proud to present a rare glimpse of the original *Dracula* ending:

AS WE LOOKED there came a terrible convulsion of the earth so that we seemed to rock to and fro and fell to our knees. At the same moment with a roar which seemed to shake the very heavens the whole castle and the rock and even the hill on which it stood seemed to rise into the air and scatter in fragments....

From where we stood it seemed as though the one fierce volcano burst had satisfied the need of nature and that the castle and the structure of the hill had sunk again into the void. We were so appalled with the suddenness and the grandeur that we forgot to think of ourselves.

Luckily, the author of *Dracula* never lived to see such unofficial "sequels" as 1999's *Zoltan: Hound of Dracula* or 2004's *Dracula 3000*, which takes place in outer space. If he could have predicted any of those awful movies, he might have killed Count Dracula on page 1!

Bat Facts

Vampire bats are creatures that really do feed on blood. This impolite habit is called hematophagy.

Only three bat species feed on blood: the common vampire bat, the hairy-legged vampire bat, and the white-winged vampire bat.

Vampire bats typically feed at night. A single bat can drink its own body weight in blood.

Their bat spit contains a substance that prevents a victim's blood from clotting too fast. The name of that substance? Draculin.

EXTRA! EXTRA!

A Serbian soldier named Arnald Paole barely survived what he believed to be a vampire attack while serving in the army. Then he returned home to the village of Meduegna—only to get crushed to death by a wagon. Thirty days after burial, villagers spotted him roaming the night, and authorities "staked" out the scene as swiftly as possible, reported Dr. Joseph Ennemoser in 1854 (who died right after!).

EXTRA! EXTRA!

In 1867 two crew members were missing aboard a Boston fishing ship. Frantically exploring every dark recess, the captain soon discovered a sailor who called himself James Brown. Brown was found feasting upon the neck of one crew member, while another bloodless soul lay nearby, according to the *Brooklyn Eagle* (November 4, 1892).

VAMPIRES IN NEW ENGLAND.

Dead Bodies Dug Up and Their Hearts Burned to Prevent Disease.

STRANGE SUPERSTITION OF LONG AGO.

The Old Belief Was that Ghostly Monsters Sucked the Blood of Their Living Relatives.

RECENT ethnological research has disclosed something very extraordinary in Rhode Island. It appears that the ancient vampire superstition still survives in that State, and within the last few years many people have been digging up the dead bodies of relatives for the purpose of burning their hearts.

Near Newport scores of such exhumations have been made, the purpose being to prevent the dead from preying upon the living. The belief entertained is that a person who has died of consumption is likely to rise from the grave at night and suck the blood of surviving members of his or her family, thus dooming them to a similar fate.

ACTUAL NEWSPAPER TEXT!
Excerpt from *The New York World*
(February 2, 1896)

WERE THESE VAMPIRES REAL?

By the 1800s, fewer and fewer people believed in vampires. Doctors and scientists were getting much better at explaining why a dead person might be mistaken for a person who is not-quite-dead. Sometimes, for example, a body decomposes in such a way that human teeth protrude like fangs. Other times, a body might come back to life because it never really died at all!

...e late nineteenth ...ury, a common word ...ampire was *nosferatu* ...(-fur-ah-too). In ...the first major ...e based on *Dracula* ...1922's *Nosferatu*: ...mphony of Horror, ...ring the peculiar Max ...eck, shown here.

Complete with garlic powder and wooden stakes, Vampire Killing Kits were said to be widely available in Eastern Europe—including Transylvania—during the 1800s. Today, they're valuable collectors' items.

$12,000

IT CAME FROM THE SEA!

FOR SAILORS OF ANY ERA, THE FEAR COMES IN WAVES.

Welcome aboard the S.S. *Horrifica*! Mind your step, locate your life jacket (just in case!), and prepare to set sail.

Oh, and one more tiny morsel of advice . . .

If you plan to go for a swim, please remember the following: In the coal-black eyes of every sea creature, we humans are merely trespassers—at best.

At worst? We're LUNCH.

Have a nice trip!

— Captain Gee

Just how vast is a halibut's habitat? Almost seventy-five percent of Earth's surface is hidden by water.

Captains and crewmen have long swapped stories of underwater teeth machines with fins. Stories of swiftly moving behemoths that appear, destroy ships, and disappear. Stories of creatures big enough to wrap their tentacles around a school bus, yet clever enough to hide from humans for centuries.

Guided by sonar tracking devices and robotic cameras, modern scientists are making new sense out of these ancient tales. A single submarine dive is far more likely to encounter "alien" life-forms than a thousand space shuttle missions. This was certainly the case in late 2004, when marine biologists caught their first good glimpse of a living giant squid. Scientists believe their slimy find once inspired Norway's myth of the ferocious Kraken. In 2006, the world was equally stunned when researchers off the coast of Papua, Indonesia, announced that they had identified a new species of shark...that walks on its fins!

As the prying eyes of science dive deeper than ever before, there's no telling what other secret monsters will be revealed.

The sperm whale is the largest toothed animal ever to inhabit Earth. In the past, decayed whale corpses have been mistaken for enormous sea serpents. Each of these so-called "globsters" (pictured) is usually revealed to be a whale's fatty tissue.

Avast, scurvy knaves! Two out of three *Pirates of the Caribbean* movies agree: The Kraken will send ya packin'. During a time when few landlubbers believed such a creature could exist, biologist Pierre Dénys de Montfort bet his entire career on the possibility that the myth of the Kraken was true. He published the above picture in 1802's *Histoire Naturelle des Mollusques*. Sadly, his peers still weren't convinced, and two decades later, he died penniless and hungry. Poor Pierre—if only he could have seen what today's marine biologists have seen! The evidence proves that something quite Kraken-like did exist back then—and still does today....

Accursed Kraken, thy true name now be known. 'Tis scrawled on the next page!

TRACKIN' THE KRAKEN

Even today, there are those who will tell you there's no such thing as sea monsters. To those wet blankets you need only shout two words: *Architeuthis dux!* No, *Architeuthis dux* is not a spell for turning humans into ducks—although it may sound like one. It's actually the scientific name for the giant squid.

If your nonbelieving friends demand proof, direct them to the Natural History Museum in London, where they might spot an *Architeuthis dux* on display, which the museum's marine biologists call Archie for short. Archie (pictured) is twenty-eight feet—roughly the same length as an oil truck.

Oh, and do ignore that chemical smell: Archie's thick mantle (upper body), eight arms, and two tentacles are preserved in a formol-saline solution. So reassure your friends that Archie is quite dead. Live specimens are ultra-rare. For decades, even the most hi-tech underwater cameras found nothing until 2004, when Japanese zoologist Tsunemi Kubodera finally hooked a tentacle more than half a mile below the water's surface. Kubodera's catch put up a courageous fight, revealing fiercer instincts than any scientist had predicted. Just how fierce is the giant squid? After four hours, the creature was so intent on escaping that it severed its own tentacle.

When Kubodera drew the eighteen-foot tentacle aboard his ship, it still slithered, blindly seeking human flesh as if it had a hungry mind of its own....

Tell your nonbelieving friends to keep that in mind as they view Archie's circular saw-like sucker rings. They'll believe in monsters then.

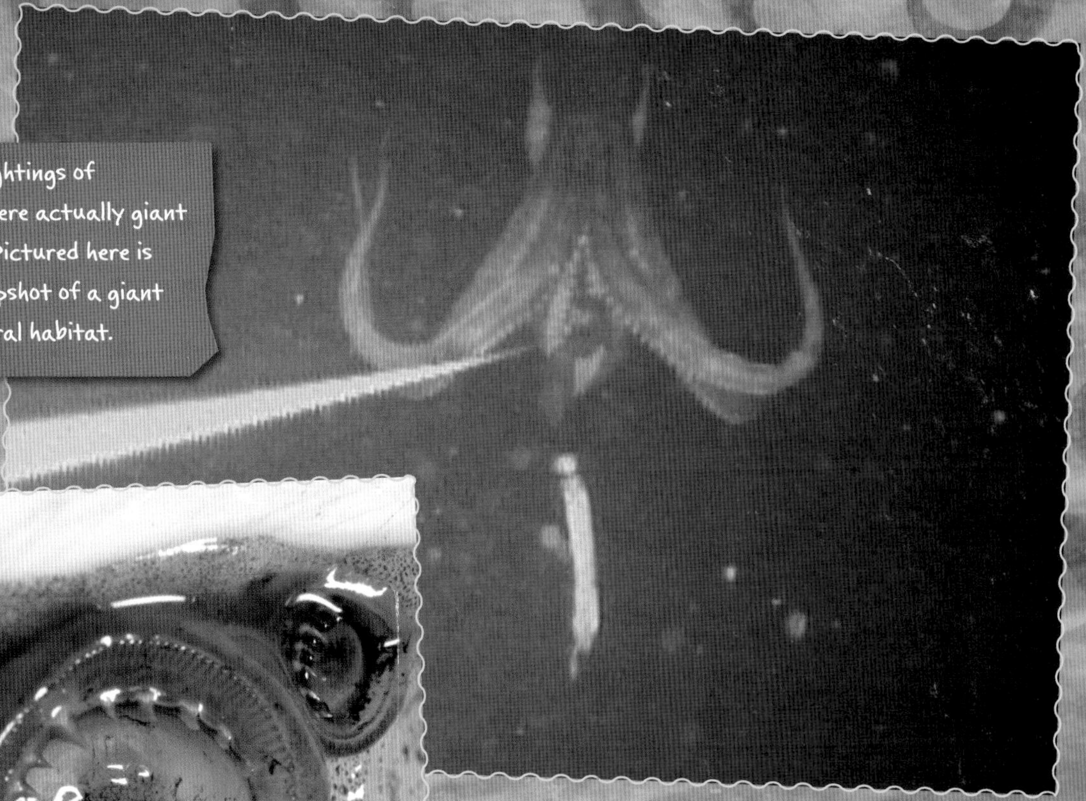

Many Kraken sightings of centuries past were actually giant squid sightings. Pictured here is a rare 2004 snapshot of a giant squid in its natural habitat.

Each giant squid tentacle has—ouch!—hundreds of jagged sucker rings.

HOW GIANT IS GIANT?

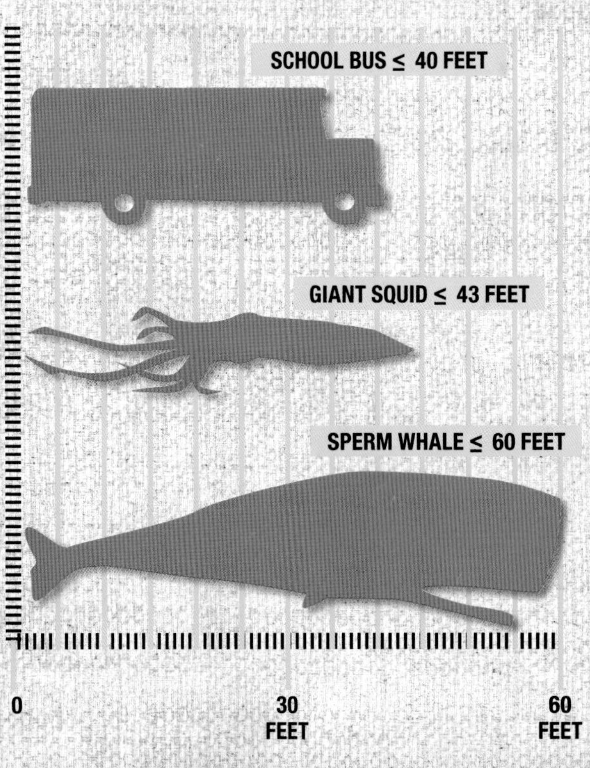

SCHOOL BUS ≤ 40 FEET

GIANT SQUID ≤ 43 FEET

SPERM WHALE ≤ 60 FEET

| 0 | 30 FEET | 60 FEET |

THE TERRIFYING TOOTH!

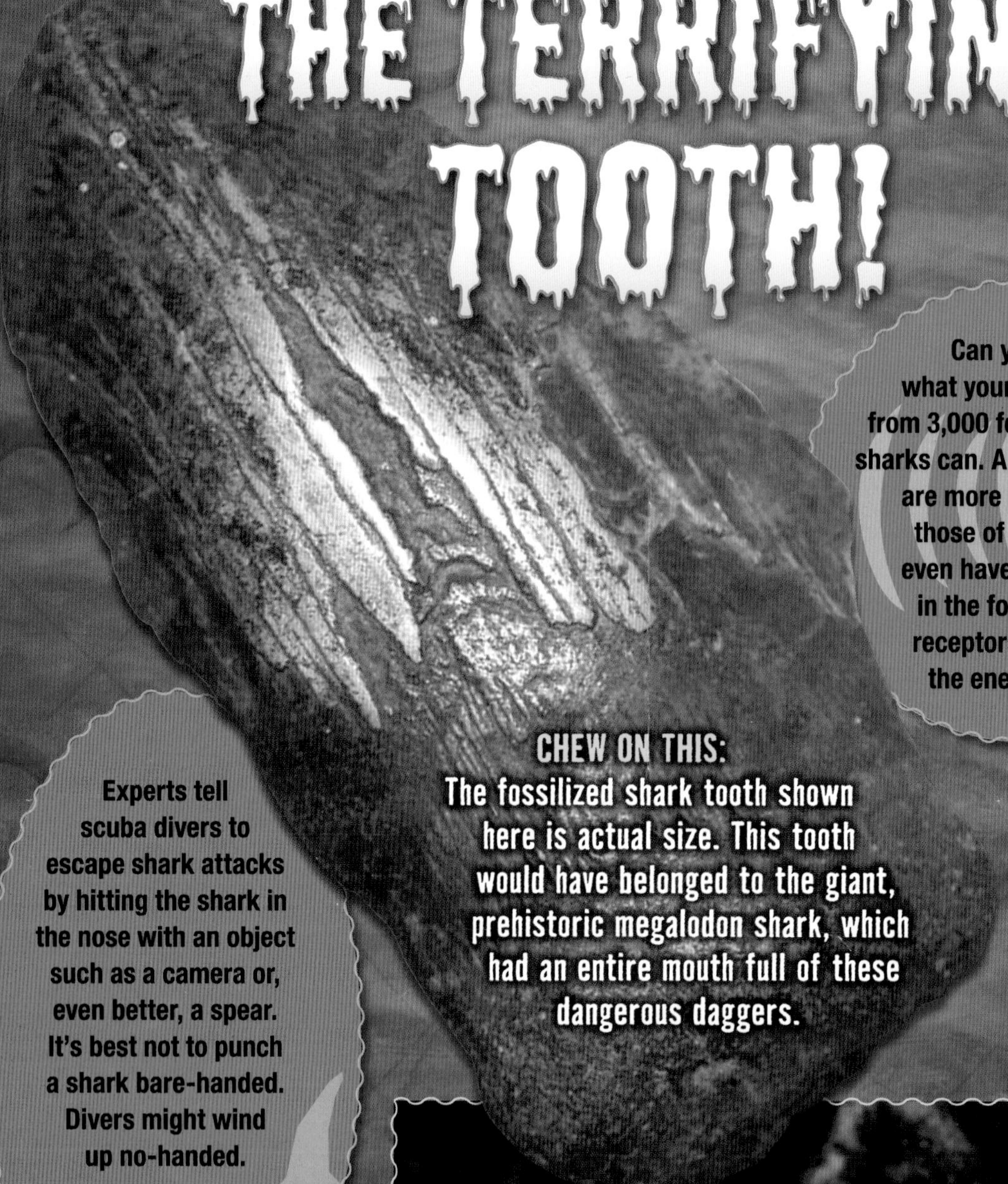

Can you hear what your victims say from 3,000 feet away? Most sharks can. All of their senses are more powerful than those of a human. They even have a "sixth sense" in the form of electrical receptors that detect the energy of prey.

CHEW ON THIS:
The fossilized shark tooth shown here is actual size. This tooth would have belonged to the giant, prehistoric megalodon shark, which had an entire mouth full of these dangerous daggers.

Experts tell scuba divers to escape shark attacks by hitting the shark in the nose with an object such as a camera or, even better, a spear. It's best not to punch a shark bare-handed. Divers might wind up no-handed.

The speckled carpet shark (*Hemiscyllium freycineti*) walks on its fins, enabling it to hunt in shallow waters.

"YOU'RE GONNA NEED A BIGGER BOAT!"

That panic-stricken movie line is from a scene in the classic fright flick *Jaws*, when the main character first catches a glimpse of the title teeth (the real stars of the show!). In *Jaws*, a tiny fishing vessel proves no match for what's prowling in the blue abyss—a great white shark. Steven Spielberg's twenty-six-foot muncher-and-cruncher—nicknamed "Bruce" by the director—was so shocking that fewer Americans went to the beach during the summer of 1975, according to reports at the time.

Now, this might be the right moment to mention that sharks are useful, graceful creatures, and in real life, they seldom attack humans. That being said, leave it to your trusty ENCYCLOPEDIA HORRIFICA to bring you one instance when they did!

When? In July of 1916. Where? Mostly in relatively shallow waters near Matawan, New Jersey. Why? Good question. Nearly a century later, nobody is certain why the "Matawan Man-Eater" attacked five swimmers in twelve days, including two twelve-year-old boys. The feeding frenzy became front-page news from coast to coast. During a time when images of sharks were not as common as they are today, people spread rumors about a monster with venom-filled fangs on the side of its head. Even the U.S. Coast Guard went after the killer shark.

Finally, a great white shark was caught in Raritan Bay with—gulp—fifteen pounds of *person* inside its stomach. The summer of 1916 haunted Jersey beachgoers for decades, inspiring author Peter Benchley later to write a novel with a now-famous title: *Jaws*.

FLYING DUTCHMAN, ARE YOU OUT THERE?

In addition to the Kraken, the *Pirates of the Caribbean* movies also re-introduced the world to another seafaring favorite: the ill-fated ghost ship known as the *Flying Dutchman*. One might say that this seemingly unrealistic tale "holds water," too.

Many versions of the story exist today, but here's the spookiest: In 1641, a mighty storm was surging off the coast of Capetown, Africa. As the waves grew higher and the wicked wind blasted his ship's sails, Captain Hendrik van der Decken, a Dutchman, shook his fist at the heavens and cursed the Creator above. He swore his ship would make it around the cape if it took him until doomsday. Bad move...

Doomsday arrived all too soon. Van der Decken and his entire crew lost their lives to the tempest, and their punishment had only just begun. Since then, many sailors have spotted the *Flying Dutchman* from afar, especially during World War II. It's been

said that no soul aboard the ship may rest until he finds another soul to take his place.

Sometimes the phantom captain still asks people to deliver written letters to the crew's long-dead loved ones. If asked, the living are advised to say no—if they value their souls.

While no phantom photos of the *Flying Dutchman* are known to exist, there are plenty of other soggy spirits out there. Seamen James Courtney and Michael Meehan became two of the most famous in December of 1924. They died on duty aboard the S.S. *Watertown*. According to crew members, the floating likenesses of both Courtney and Meehan appeared again and again for many days thereafter—so frequently, in fact, that Captain Keith Tracy purchased a camera and took six photos. The sixth and most intriguing exposure is featured here.

SPECIAL INVESTIGATION

SUBJECT: The Feejee Mermaid
MISSION: To learn the true history of a famous fake
IN SEARCH OF: The original 165-year-old "mermaid"
LOCATION: The Barnum Museum
(www.barnum-museum.org)
MEMO TO HEADQUARTERS: Little girls are made of sugar and spice and everything nice. Little mermaids? You'll be sorry you asked.

BRIDGEPORT, CONNECTICUT—"Want to see our beautiful girl?" asks Deb Rose, Director of Education at the Barnum Museum, named after famous showman and circus founder P. T. Barnum.

Although the Barnum Museum doesn't get too crowded nowadays, people had to wait in long lines to see this "beautiful girl" a century and a half ago. Like Walt Disney's *The Little Mermaid*, Barnum's version had green scales and a lengthy tail. Only Barnum's creature didn't sing or smile; it simply lay there, hideous and dead. She had been cobbled together from the severed pieces of a fish and two or more primates.

"Barnum's genius was taking some act or something that was not all that exceptional, and creating a stir about it so that people wanted to see it," says Ms. Rose. "He was a genius at creating demand."

How did he do this? Partly through advertising. Ticket buyers were lured by false pictures of lovely mermaids that hardly resembled what they were about to see.

The specimen at the Barnum Museum is certainly worth the price of admission, her hands and face frozen for eternity in a strange expression that mimics shock. However, Ms. Rose explains that their Feejee Mermaid is merely an artist's reproduction of the original. That is to say, it's a fake of a fake!

Determined to track down the slippery little fiend, ENCYCLOPEDIA HORRIFICA also contacted the Coney Island Circus Sideshow, based on a "tip" from a sword swallower.

"We exhibited a phony Feejee Mermaid years back," explains Dick Zigun, President of Coney Island USA organization. "We no longer have it."

Further research reveals that the original might have perished during one of two fires in the 1800s. Other reports suggest that another antique "mermaid" located in Cambridge, Massachusetts, might have been Barnum's.

Among fans of fake mercreatures, only one thing is certain: Other specimens began appearing in circuses and sideshows from coast to coast after Barnum's hit the big time. So an old, dried-up "mermaid" could surface in almost any city—even yours.

X-ray of a Feejee Mermaid.

The Beasts of Barnum

"Barnum called himself the 'Prince of Humbug,'" says Ms. Rose when discussing the Feejee Mermaid. "'Humbug' is an old-fashioned word that means a fake or a trick." Can you guess which of these other creatures were real—and which were "humbugs"? Turn to page 135 for the answers.

A. The Cardiff Giant
B. Jumbo the Elephant
C. Tom Thumb the Dwarf Elephant
D. The Man-Eating Chicken

Will the real Feejee Mermaid please stand up? Or at least . . . wiggle her tail? One replica (above) is on display at the Barnum Museum in Bridgeport, Connecticut. A much older specimen (below) is owned by the Harvard Peabody Museum in Cambridge, Massachusetts. Although neither one of these bathing beauties was ever a true mercreature, some researchers believe the one below is the same one that P. T. Barnum put on display in 1842.

SEA AND BE SEEN

Merpeople may look outlandish to the science-savvy readers of today, but eyewitness reports have been flopping around for centuries.

Even your history teacher probably doesn't know the following mer-data about Christopher Columbus: On January 9, 1493, while exploring the Americas, he matter-of-factly described three mermaids in his captain's log. He stated that it was not the first time he'd witnessed such creatures.

In the village of Zennor in Cornwall, England, a centuries-old myth describes a mermaid who enchanted a lad named Mathew Trewella—or perhaps it was the other way around. Upon hearing Mathew's voice in the church choir, the mermaid emerged from the sea to listen closely to his song, day after day, and ultimately proclaimed her love for him. Then Mathew disappeared. The end. Townsfolk never saw him again.

Far more bizarre are records of the bishop-fish and the monk-fish. The stubborn bishop-fish (pictured) was supposedly captured near Germany in 1531. As an act of protest, it refused to eat and died from starvation after three days. The monk-fish, also described around that time, earned its name by looking like a bald monk in a robe. It was supposedly caught off the coast of Denmark.

Japanese folklore describes a similar monklike creature—the *umibōzu*. Boatmen were carefully trained to ward off the *umibōzu* by performing a ritualistic dance on deck that involved a lot of red streamers. Nobody knows what effect it had on actual bald monks.

Creatures mistaken for "merpeople" include manatee, seals, and dolphins.

Townsfolk claim a mermaid once visited Zennor Church in Cornwall, England. They carved her likeness in this bench where she supposedly listened to Mr. Mathew Trewella sing in the choir.

ALIEN INVASION!

ATTENTION, PEOPLE OF EARTH: QUICK! LOOK UP!

Want proof of alien life? Keep your eyes on the skies.

At least, that's what most ufologists believe. Ufologists study unidentified flying objects, better known as UFOs. Of course, everybody sees objects in the sky that are hard to identify. That's to be expected. Every year, ufologists look at photos and video footage featuring hundreds of zooming dots. Do all zooming dots come from Planet X? Let's hope not.

However . . . if you look outside your window long enough, you just might witness a zooming dot that seems different from all the rest—the shape, the movement, the strange glow, everything about it.

If you see one of those zooming dots, take a picture—fast. Zooming dots don't have all day, you know!

Study the snapshots thoughtfully before jumping to any conclusions. Good ufologists are always careful about what they do or don't label as "extraterrestrial," or otherworldly. Before they try to figure out what something is, they have to figure out what it *isn't*. So ask a few questions about your UFO photo: Could that odd little dot be an airplane? A distant bird? A nearby insect?

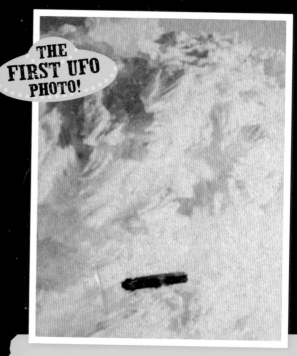

THE FIRST UFO PHOTO!

During the winter of 1870–1871, a New Hampshire resident captured this image of a rocket-shaped object flying by a cloudy mountaintop. Unless you had wings or a hot-air balloon, back then there was no (earthly) way to fly.

The answers will require further research. (Answers usually do.) Meanwhile, as you cross off the plane, the bird, and the insect, add one other possibility to the list. Somewhere in the sky, a UFO could be pointing a camera right at *YOU*.

The question is, **Why?**

Judging by some theories, Earth has always been a popular vacation destination for aliens.

4 BILLION YEARS AGO

Achoo! Some scientists believe that microscopic germs from outer space were among the first organisms on Earth. They call this theory *panspermia*.

PREHISTORIC TIMES

In Southern France and Northern Spain, ancient cave paintings depict woolly mammoths, boars, and floating discs.

On May 11, 1950, Paul Trent, a respected farmer and family man, took this photo near McMinnville, Oregon. A few weeks later, Mr. Trent and his wife received a knock on their door: It was a U. S. Air Force investigator. Neither the air force nor the Trents' neighbors could cite any reason why the Trents would lie.

CLOSE ENCOUNTER: THE FIRST KIND

On June 24, 1947, several UFOs allegedly zipped by Kenneth Arnold as he piloted his plane above Washington State. Nine UFOs, in fact! Ever since Arnold's "flying saucers" first became national news, so many sightings have taken place that ufologists now divide them into seven kinds of "Close Encounter."

A Close Encounter of the First Kind describes a sighting of a distant UFO. Although Arnold took no photos of his Close Encounter of the First Kind, many other UFOs are captured on film every year. Some are obvious fakes. Others are harder to explain.

For many decades, earthlings in Mexico and the American Southwest have witnessed more UFOs than anybody else. One of the most perplexing Close Encounters of the First Kind allegedly occurred in Mexico City on August 6, 1997. Nearly thirty seconds of video footage were captured before the object departed into the hazy horizon.

5,000 YEARS AGO

The Great Pyramid of Egypt is created by intelligent life-forms from outer space, according to some claims.

2,300 YEARS AGO

In the Middle East, two "flying shields" spit lightning at Alexander the Great's army, according to records at the time.

1100 AD

Islanders—or aliens, according to some—carve the first of nearly 900 humanoid statues on Easter Island in the Pacific Ocean.

CASE FILE:
THE MYSTERY OF THE FUSED SAND
APRIL 24, 1964

If you can figure out who—or what—landed in Socorro, New Mexico, then you've outsmarted many a ufologist before you.

Lonnie Zamora, a respected police officer, was about to pull over a speeding driver when a loud sound thundered in the desert. Around 5:45 P.M., Zamora let the speeder go and chased the sound instead. Soon, he spotted what he thought was an overturned car. As he drove closer, it looked less like a car . . . and more like a white, egg-shaped UFO.

That's not all. Alongside the aircraft, he noticed two figures wearing white jumpsuits. "About the size of boys," he later said. Startled, one of them turned its head directly toward Zamora!

As Zamora got out of his vehicle, the two figures got back into theirs—and quickly achieved liftoff.

Scorched plant material and unusual substances were later discovered on the scene. The most unique evidence was the melted sand found there. It was located where the UFO's after-burners allegedly had been.

Later, a U.S. Air Force investigator would write, "This is the best-documented case on record, and still we have been unable, in spite of thorough investigation, to find the vehicle or other stimulus that scared Zamora to the point of panic."

Ufologists once blamed "crop circles" on artistic aliens. Today, most are thought to be human hoaxes.

APRIL 1561

Several round objects reportedly swoop through the skies over Nuremberg, Germany. In 1566, it happens again, in Switzerland.

APRIL 1897

Popular Astronomy, The New York Sun, and other publications describe a wave of coast-to-coast "airship" sightings that peak around this time.

1906

Astronomer Percival Lowell publishes Mars and Its Canals. Using telescopes, he deduces that Martians built complex waterways!

Shh! Don't tell anybody: You are looking at a rare satellite image of an ultrasecret military base in the Nevada desert. It goes by names like Groom Lake, Dreamland, or, most often, Area 51. Some satellite images reveal entrances to underground bunkers, plus the longest runway in the world. (Six-mile runways come in handy when testing supersonic spy planes.) Many ufologists believe that Area 51 has also housed UFOs like the one that allegedly crashed at Roswell.

HALLOWEEN EVE 1938

More than a million people panic in the streets after listening to a radio adaptation of the novel *The War of the Worlds*. Turn to page 116 for more.

JUNE 24, 1947

The Kenneth Arnold Incident— To describe this UFO sighting, newspapers make up the now-famous phrase "flying saucer," but Arnold never said it.

JULY 2, 1947

Something crash-lands in Roswell, New Mexico. Decades later, earthling tourists will also land there— in search of T-shirts and souvenirs.

CASE FILE:
THE MOST FAMOUS UFO EVER
JULY 3, 1947

The world-famous Roswell Incident is much more than a UFO story. Slowly, it has become a modern myth, passed down from one generation to the next.

Here are the facts: One night in 1947, near Roswell, New Mexico, rancher William "Mac" Brazel heard an eerie explosion. He didn't investigate until sunrise. Days later, on July 8, the *Roswell Daily Record* published a story about what Brazel found that morning: strange debris stretching over three-quarters of a mile.

The very next day, the paper followed up with a headline that told an entirely different story: "Gen. Ramey Empties Roswell Saucer." It referred to Major General Roger Ramey, who claimed the

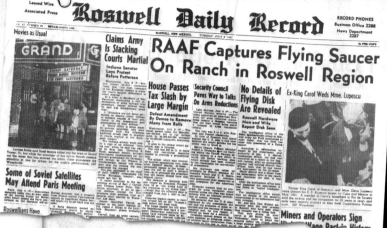

wreckage was nothing more than a balloon designed to test the weather. The U.S. military stuck to that story for a long time.

The saucer myth didn't really take off until decades later, when supposed eyewitnesses began telling their own versions. They added some surprising twists—details like indestructible metal and secret military bases and even doomed alien passengers.

Over the years, the U.S. government has "emptied" the saucer myth again and again. Long ago, they told ufologists about Project Mogul, a secret spy technology first tested in 1947. This was what actually crashed at Roswell, argued the officials.

Many locals still claim otherwise. The most convincing of these supposed witnesses? Mortician Glenn Dennis. He says the Roswell Army Air Field (RAAF) asked him to supply several small coffins two days after the crash.

Roswell today: The tourists have landed!

1951

An officer in the U.S. Air Force creates a new phrase: Unidentified Flying Object, or UFO.

1952

The air force begins the top-secret Project Blue Book, collecting 12,618 UFO reports over the next seventeen years.

APRIL 24, 1964

At 5:45 P.M. in New Mexico, Lonnie Zamora witnesses a grounded UFO—and two tiny passengers. The evidence puzzles even the air force.

CLOSE ENCOUNTER: THE FOURTH* KIND

> * A form of kidnapping in which the kidnappers are aliens.

Travis Walton's boss based this drawing on Mr. Walton's eyewitness account.

CASE FILE:
ABDUCTED BY THE LIGHT
NOVEMBER 5, 1975

After a long day of woodcutting in an Arizona national forest, Travis Walton, age 22, climbed into a big pickup truck with six other men. If you believe all six of Walton's coworkers, they were about to become eyewitnesses to a **Close Encounter of the Fourth Kind**.

As night fell on the forest, their truck didn't get very far before a glowing, disc-shaped object appeared nearby. It hovered only fifteen or twenty feet above the ground, glowing like a giant ghost. The truck slowly moved forward. So did the UFO, carefully gliding through the trees.

Walton was curious—perhaps too curious. He got out of the vehicle and raced toward the light. Soon after, a bluish-green tractor beam shot him in the chest, lifting him many feet into the air.

Nobody saw Travis Walton again for five whole days.

Late on the evening of November 10, Walton was discovered at a gas station, ten pounds thinner and unshaven. He thought he'd only been gone a few hours!

Like any so-called "alien abduction," Walton's might have been made up. He did fail a lie detector test. Yet he passed two others. All of his coworkers believed they'd witnessed an extraterrestrial event, too. Weirdest of all? When Walton returned, two doctors examined him, and they said his bodily fluids were normal, as though *something* had kept him alive all that time in the freezing-cold forest.

Something unidentified to this day . . .

I. WITNESS

The handsome, jaw-dropping skull on the front of this book is a useful reminder: Your eyes can play tricks on you. Many "optical illusions" are mistaken for alien spacecraft every year.

Weather balloons

The planet Venus

Swamp gas

Hi-tech military aircraft

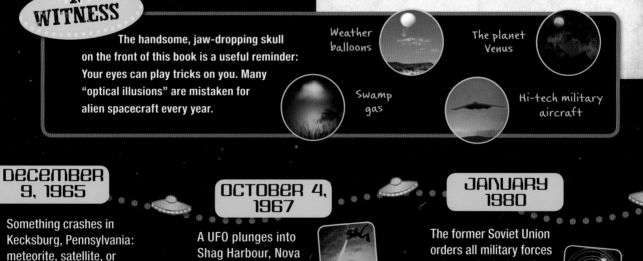

DECEMBER 9, 1965

Something crashes in Kecksburg, Pennsylvania: meteorite, satellite, or doomed alien flight?

OCTOBER 4, 1967

A UFO plunges into Shag Harbour, Nova Scotia. The Canadian government officially launches a secret underwater investigation.

JANUARY 1980

The former Soviet Union orders all military forces to be on the lookout for UFOs. The order lasts for thirteen years.

A Hoax Is No Joke, Folks

Hoaxes. Call them "Uncool Fake-Outs," but don't call them UFOs. Ufologists must always beware of sneaky earthlings who intentionally mislead others.

ENCYCLOPEDIA HORRIFICA has identified one such case to be the "alien cemetery" in Aurora, Texas. Sure, you're probably thinking, *Aliens? Cemeteries? Beam me up...to Texas!* Well, don't take to the sky just yet. True, a cemetery does exist on Cemetery Road in Aurora. Is an alien buried there? Probably not.

This tale can be traced back to April 19, 1897, when the *Dallas Morning News* made an April Fool of every reader. Prank-pulling reporter S. E. Haydon wrote about a demolished "airship" and its soon-to-be-buried pilot, who "was not an inhabitant of this world."

In 1973, ufologists interviewed several long-time residents in order to get their first-hand perspectives. One witness in her eighties said she remembered this event to be a hoax. Another man agreed, according to the Wise County Historical Commission.

* Any form of direct communication between earthlings and alien life-forms.

CASE FILE:
THE (VERY) LONG-DISTANCE CALL
AUGUST 15, 1977

In May of 1977, *Star Wars* taught moviegoers how to speak like alien Wookiees. Just a few months later, scientists learned what a true alien might sound like. It was all thanks to a SETI lab in Ohio. (SETI means Search for Extraterrestrial Intelligence.) Throughout the world, SETI researchers transmit special radio signals into space using radar dishes the size of volcanoes. Then, they wait (and wait!) for a response. That summer, they got what seemed like one. A researcher was so excited that he famously wrote the word "Wow!" on the computer printout. Alas, the signal was much, much quieter than Chewbacca, and it didn't mean anything in any human language. So SETI labs continue hunting for life "in a galaxy far, far away."

Although many unidentified airships (like the one on page 20) did appear during the late 1800s, Aurora wasn't on their flight plan.

DECEMBER 29, 1980

An enormous, diamond-shaped UFO hovers above a road near Dayton, Texas, say three witnesses. Then, more than twenty helicopters arrive to chase it.

JUNE 12, 1998

A flying metallic object nearly collides with a passenger jet leaving London, according to the British Civil Aviation Authority.

MAY 17, 1999

The computer program, SETI@home, launches online. Want to join the Search for Extraterrestrial Intelligence? Visit http://setiathome.berkeley.edu

CLOSE ENCOUNTER: THE SIXTH* KIND

CASE FILE:
AN ALIEN DEATH-RAY?
JANUARY 7, 1948

* Any contact with an alien life-form that results in the death of an animal or human being.

In most UFO cases, aliens pose little threat to humans. One exception is the case of Captain Thomas Mantell, Jr., whose F-51 fighter plane put up quite a fight chasing a UFO, then crashed.

On the day of Mantell's demise, Kentucky was abuzz with UFO reports. Already in the sky due to a training mission, Mantell and two other pilots were sent to investigate the sighting. At 14,000 feet, the planes went into what's called "maximum climb"—straight up at 180 miles-per-hour. At 22,000 feet, oxygen becomes less plentiful and the air more difficult to breathe. By that point, two of the pilots gave up and turned around, but not Mantell. He

kept going up. He had the UFO in his sights. . . .

What happened next is uncertain. His watch stopped forty-five minutes later, at 3:18 P.M. Officials knew this because they found it amid the plane's wreckage. Did Mantell simply run out of oxygen? It's likely.

Nonetheless, Kentucky residents who witnessed the UFO from the ground didn't think so. Maybe whatever he was chasing didn't want to be chased, some said.

Much like the Roswell Incident during the same time period, the Mantell Incident was eventually blamed on a hi-tech balloon. Still, many ufologists doubt that a trained pilot would identify a balloon as anything other than a balloon. . . .

CLOSE ENCOUNTER: THE SEVENTH KIND

Leaving the most horrific for last, ufologists say a Close Encounter of the Seventh Kind is when visitors from outer space create alien-human hybrids. It's difficult to imagine why an extraterrestrial species might wish to create such ghastly creatures. Perhaps aliens just like science projects.

On the bright side, no good evidence of hybrids exists in real life—only on TV. *The X-Files* portrays aliens as intergalactic Dr. Frankensteins whose goal is to create enough hybrids to colonize Earth. Of course, *The X-Files* is science fiction and not science fact, so you won't find Close Encounters of the Seventh Kind in any textbook.

Not in any textbook on Earth, at least.

WELCOME!

JANUARY 2005

The Journal of the British Interplanetary Society reports that alien visitations are (a) possible and (b) very likely, according to astrophysicists.

LATE 2000

The National Aviation Reporting Center on Anomalous Phenomena begins investigating pilots' so-called Unidentified Aerial Phenomena (UAP).

AUGUST 2002

Roper poll: Almost half of Americans believe Earth has been visited by aliens. Nearly as many believe aliens might be watching us right now!

BELIEVE

HOWLING at the MOON!

A Human's Guide to Werewolves

Throughout human (and not-so-human) history, there have always been rumors of "shape-shifters"—those beings that can transform from one creature into another. Werewolves are the most vicious of shape-shifters, clawing their way from forest trail to city sidewalk by the light of the full moon.

Folklore teaches us that a single bite or scratch from a werewolf is often all it takes to turn you into one forever. Believe it or not, some people actually choose to become werewolves

Lycanthropy
(*lie-CAN-throw-pea*)
is a medical term. It describes a rare mental illness that causes you to mistake yourself for a wolf.

on purpose. According to Russian tradition, an ancient chant will usually do the trick (see below). Europeans are said to prefer a messier method: It involves ordinary wolf fur and a few simple household ingredients like parsley and the fat of a human child.

Before you begin shopping for either of those items, keep in mind the fate of a shape-shifter: If you're half wolf, you're all bad. Your rage becomes your only friend.

Nothing can stop a werewolf except dawn or death. Whichever comes first.

Bullet Points

- What's the best way to kill a werewolf? Silver bullets, according to recent movies and TV shows.

- Older, more trustworthy sources like *The Book of Were-Wolves* (1865) say very little on the subject of silver. Take no chances: Use it anyway!

- Some say the Beast of Gévaudan (see p. 30) was finally killed by a silver bullet. Others disagree. The rifle remains in France, the bullet lost.

WARNING! ## ANCIENT WEREWOLF CHANT* **DON'T READ THIS.**

Only because no book would be complete without an Ancient Werewolf Chant, ENCYCLOPEDIA HORRIFICA offers one right here.

*In the ocean sea, on the island Buyan,
in the open plain,
shines the moon upon an aspen stump,
into the green wood, into the spreading vale.
Around the stump goes a shaggy wolf;
under his teeth are all the horned cattle;
but into the wood the wolf goes not;
in the vale the wolf does not roam.
Moon, moon! Gold-horned moon!
Melt the bullet, blunt the knife, rot the cudgel,
strike fear into man, beast, and reptile,
so that they may not seize the gray wolf,
nor tear from him his warm hide.
My word is firm, firmer than sleep
or the strength of heroes.*

* Adapted from *Songs of the Russian People* (1872), by W. R. S. Ralston, who does not explain how to become human again!

A Werewolf's Guide to Werewolves

Welcome, werewolves. For the first time, enjoy something written just for you! In the interest of fair and balanced reporting, this page is here to remind you of your long and proud history.

In some Hollywood movies nowadays, werewolves are also known as lycanthropes (or lycans, for short). That certainly beats a name like *The Wolf-Man*, the title of the first major movie to star a werewolf.

Let us know which name you prefer. We humans are here to help — just as long as you don't help yourselves to us!

Approximate age of the first story ever written, which featured the werewolf-like Enkidu:

4,000 years old

Lycanthropy
(grr-RRR-rrr-rrrh!)
dates back to 1584 AD. Originally, the word described people who were thought to be *actual* werewolves.

Number of big-screen werewolf movies "sighted" since 1941's *The Wolf-Man*:

More than 220 films

HISTORY'S HAIRIEST

The ancient Greeks spoke of **Lycaon**, a wicked ruler who planned to murder Zeus. If planning to murder the king of all Greek gods, it's important to succeed. Lycaon did not, and Zeus turned him into a wolf.

The word *berserk* comes from the Norse *berserkir*, fierce medieval warriors who wore wolf skins over their armor. Were the *berserkir* able to shape-shift? Not many of their enemies survived long enough to find out.

Little Red Riding Hood told the **Big Bad Wolf**, "Grandmother, what big teeth you have!" It was the last thing she ever said—at least in the original 1697 version of this famous fairy tale. In the modern version, she survives without a scratch.

Number of werewolf sightings reported in France between 1520 and 1630:

30,000 sightings

WHO'S AFRAID OF THE BIG, BAD WOLF? ALL OF FRANCE!

Once upon a time, Gévaudan was a district in Southern France best known for its delicious cheeses. By the summer of 1764, it was best known for its delicious *villagers*—if you were the so-called Beast of Gévaudan, that is.

The Beast—an enormous, wolflike predator—is as much a mystery today as it was in the 1700s. The first victim on record was fourteen-year-old Jeanne Boulet. Around June 30, 1764, Ms. Boulet was herding sheep in a lush meadow. Some twigs snapped in the distance. "Who's there?" she reportedly asked. Alas, the Beast was there: over 130 pounds of lean muscle, sharp teeth, and putrid-smelling fur. Strangely, it went after Jeanne and ignored the sheep!

According to an old text by investigator Abbé Pourcher, the Beast of Gévaudan was unlike a wolf in other ways, too. It was reddish-brown with a black stripe running down its back. It could pounce thirty feet, and some witnesses said they even saw it walking upright, using only its two hind legs!

Long sticks and angry words were not enough to stop the Beast.

"Parlez-vous loup-garou?"

That's French for "Do you speak werewolf?" Many moons ago, France was the werewolf capital of the world, partly because criminals were often accused of lycanthropy.

Paris, 1598: The trial of a man found half naked and hairy at a crime scene

Dole, 1573: Gilles Garnier accused of being hungry like a wolf

F R A N C E

Poligny, 1521: Three suspects confess to being a pack of wolves

Landes, 1604: Alleged "teen wolf" Jean Grenier accused of attacking girls

By now, you might be wondering if the Beast of Gévaudan was a real-life *loup-garou*, or werewolf. Many townsfolk certainly thought so.

Several victims later, the King of France dispatched some of his finest hunters, and the Beast of Gévaudan was confirmed dead in October 1764. Of course, it was also confirmed dead in April 1765 and once again in September 1765. Did it keep coming back to life? Probably not. Most historians think there were actually several creatures.

Either way, the Beast of Gévaudan finally met its match on June 19, 1767. Gray-haired hunter Jean Chastel looked the creature in the eye as he calmly readied his musket. Suddenly, Chastel ended three years of terror with a single pull of his trigger. According to some reports, Chastel then stood with the creature at his feet and whispered, "Beast, thou wilt kill no more."

The wise old woodsman was correct. Gévaudan never cried *loup-garou* again.

MONSTER MASH

THE FUR'S ABOUT TO FLY!
NO MATTER WHO WINS,
WE ALL LOSE.

HOLLYWOOD'S WEREWOLF	VERSUS	HISTORY'S WEREWOLF
Roughly six feet tall. That was the actual height of Lon Chaney (above), famous star of *The Wolf-Man*.	SIZE	Roughly six feet long, from snout to tail. Some said the Beast of Gévaudan was as big as a cow.
Timeless	TIME PERIOD	July 3, 1764 to June 19, 1767
One*	NUMBER OF VICTIMS	One hundred
Larry	NICKNAME	The Scourge
The foggy, moonlit forests of a fictitious village in the United Kingdom	FAVORITE HANGOUTS	The poverty-stricken villages of Gévaudan, now known as Lozère
Wolfsbane flowers	FAVORITE FOODS	Children who speak French
Soft and fluffy	FUR	Thick and often bullet-proof
Yes! For proof, see 1943's *Frankenstein Meets the Wolf Man*.	HAS IT MET FRANKENSTEIN'S MONSTER?	Unlikely. The Beast was real; Frankenstein's monster was not.
Ability to grow lots of hair really, really fast	STRENGTHS	A menacing mix of teeth, speed, and ferocity
Any pointy objects made of silver—especially bullets	WEAKNESSES	An insatiable hunger for human flesh
The usual mobs of superstitious peasants with torches	ENEMIES	Courageous hunter Jean Chastel, real-life slayer of monsters

*The title character claims only one human life in 1941's *The Wolf-Man*.

What attacked Gévaudan, France?

To find some answers to 200-year-old questions, ENCYCLOPEDIA HORRIFICA caught up with Professor Rolf Peterson, a leading wolf expert, in the woods of Isle Royale, Michigan. "It is not common for wolves to attack humans," explains Professor Peterson. When it comes to ordinary wolves, humans' biggest mistake is "probably an unreasonable fear of the animal." Of course, Gévaudan was attacked by no ordinary wolf, so Professor Peterson shares his thoughts on popular theories.

THE THEORY	THE WOLF EXPERT
It was a rare prehistoric animal that somehow survived extinction.	"Very doubtful."
It was a hyena.	"Way out of their African range."
It was a hybrid: part wolf and part dog.	"Certainly possible."
It was a good-wolf-gone-bad, due to a disease called rabies.	"Also very possible."

Jurassic Bark

My scientific name is *Thylacinus cynocephalus*!

In 1993's *Jurassic Park* and its sequels, modern-day scientists create ferocious dinosaur clones using fossilized blood. Most people think this is impossible in real life. But is it really? Australian researchers are creating something called the International Thylacine Specimen Database (ITSD). The purpose of this project is to clone a meat-eating marsupial that's been extinct for seventy years! This lucky animal is called the Tasmanian wolf, or thylacine. If scientists can find enough well-preserved skins and skeletons, then they may have the genetic material they need to turn Australia's lone wolf into a clone wolf.

Full-Moon Fever

Although Petrus Gonsalvus may look like a werewolf in this 1580 portrait, he is 100 percent human. He was born with a rare medical condition known as *hypertrichosis universalis,* which means "hair everywhere." Today, the condition affects only two or three families in the entire world. Researchers hope it might lead to a solution for baldness some day.

As any lycan chaser can tell you, a full moon is bad news. It's the best time to find an Extra-Extra-Large dog collar—and fast. But could there be any truth to these beliefs about the effects of the moon? Nobody knows for sure.

In recent years, some researchers have argued that a full moon actually causes humans to act wild, too. In 1978, psychologist Arnold Leiber published a book called *The Lunar Effect: Biological Tides and Human Emotions.* After carefully studying police records in Miami and Cleveland, he discovered that people committed more crimes during the full moon and the new moon. However, for every study like his, there's another one that suggests no connection at all.

And what about wolves? Well, Professor Peterson, the wolf expert, says he's seen no evidence that a full moon can lead to bad animal behavior.

The Strange Case of Mr. W

According to a 1975 medical journal, "Mr. W" was the fake name that doctors gave to one 37-year-old patient. Mr. W probably didn't want to reveal his real name because he had a few quirks. For starters, he liked to grow his beard long—really, *really* long. He also slept in cemeteries and howled at the moon. Mysteriously, medical tests revealed that the nerves in his brain seemed to malfunction only during the full moon. True lunacy!

HORRIBLE HALVES!

THE AMERICAN WERE-MOTH

In 1961, and then again in 1966 and 1967, witnesses in West Virginia spotted a tall humanoid with huge wings and bright red circles for eyes. It could even fly! Some people say it was all a hoax; others say that local owls, not giant moths, were to blame. Yet that doesn't explain other flighty sightings like the "winged human form" reported by *The New York Sun* in 1877.

THE CAMBODIAN WERE-TIGER

Even though *were-* means "man," women can become were-creatures, too. In Cambodia, for example, legend says a woman may become half tiger by smearing her entire body with a powerful ointment. Next, she must relax in the forest for a while. Seven days later, she'll return a changed woman.

THE GREEK WERE-BULL

The wolfman Lycaon isn't the only ancient Greek figure with a furry tale to tell. Another was the Minotaur, an accursed monster with a man's body but a bull's head and tail. The Minotaur dwelled in a terrifying maze beneath the palace of Minos in Crete. Just a myth? Maybe not. In the early 1900s, British archaeologist Arthur Evans located Crete and dug up an ancient palace containing mazelike passages and many paintings of bulls.

THE INDONESIAN WERE-HOBBIT

In 2003, researchers in Flores, Indonesia, dug up what they consider to be a new species of human. Dubbed *Homo floresiensis*—a.k.a. "Hobbit-man"—each prehistoric skeleton was only three feet tall…just like the mini men in J. R. R. Tolkien's *The Lord of the Rings*. Some scientists think these individuals weren't "half Hobbit" at all. Instead, the bones might have belonged to ordinary humans with microcephaly, a brain disorder that stunts growth. It's highly unlikely that diggers will find any other evidence suggesting Hobbits—such as glowing swords or magical gold rings—but Tolkien fans can always hope for the best.

Part Two

If you've ever been to a sleepover, then you already know there are quite a few ghost stories to be told. Happy phantoms. Sad phantoms. Courteous spooks and angry specters. Even some four-legged critters, adorably dead.

We here at ENCYCLOPEDIA HORRIFICA find that it can be quite a hassle keeping track of them all. Truly a logistical *nightmare!* The only way to make sense of them all is to file one's phantoms under two separate headings:

1. "Phantoms of Legend," passed from one generation to the next. (You'll often hear about these spirits in hushed tones by the flickering light of a campfire.)
2. "Fact-Based Phantoms," supported by eyewitness accounts and other forms of evidence.

In the pages ahead, you'll meet the most spectacular luminaries from both file piles.

To any ghost you see, simply point, smile, and say,

"That's the Spirit!"

BEWARE OF GHOSTS

A FATAL PHANTOM HAUNTS THE HISTORY BOOKS IN TENNESSEE.

Only one ghost on record has proven impossible for ENCYCLOPEDIA HORRIFICA to categorize. Was the so-called "Bell Witch" fact or fiction? Perhaps you can help us decide.

Until then, let's file this ghoulish gal under *M*. It stands for MURDER.

An 1894 illustration of Betsy Bell, an ordinary schoolgirl allegedly targeted by a ghost.

1.

THE LEGEND: Prior to his untimely demise in 1820 (more on that later!), a man by the name of John Bell lived with his family in a log cabin near the Red River in Robertson County, Tennessee.

THE TRUTH: "Yes, John Bell and his wife Lucy and nine children lived here," says historian Yolanda Reid, who works at the Robertson County Archives. "There are estate entries in the will books from when he died. There are deed records for the division of his land."

The Bell Homestead: What happened here in 1820?

2.

THE LEGEND: The family's woes began in 1817. Mr. Bell was enjoying a stroll in his cornfield when he encountered "a strange animal." At the time, he assumed it was an unfriendly dog. Little did he know that it would be the first of several bizarre beasts to herald the arrival of a nuisance far worse.

THE TRUTH: In folklore, many types of animals—especially black hounds—are said to be death omens. So it's possible that these creatures were connected to the coming death of Mr. Bell. It's also possible that the appearances were a mere coincidence. Stories about ghost dogs existed in the South during that period, just as they do now. Because of these stories, the Bell family might have remembered ordinary animals as "ghost animals" after things took a turn for the spooky later on.

3.

THE LEGEND: Soon after that, the family began hearing unusual noises inside the house: thumping, nibbling, and then a woman's voice. Finally, the ghost made her grand debut before family members and, later, curiosity seekers from all over. Calling herself "Kate," she could be nice at times, reportedly carrying on long conversations about the latest gossip in the tiny rural town. She could be mischievous, too, though. Mr. Bell's daughter Betsy, barely a teen, was ruthlessly bullied, her hair pulled and her face slapped by the ghost on several occasions. After that, Kate set her sights on Mr. Bell. Or so the story goes.

THE TRUTH: Although more than a dozen books have been written about the Bell Witch, most knowledge of her can be traced back to only one, *An Authenticated History of the Bell Witch* (1894), by Martin Van Buren Ingram. Take note: It was written seventy-five years after the events allegedly took place, and some historians believe it might have been a hoax. Also, the author claimed he based it on an 1846 diary written by a Bell family member who was not much older than six at the time of the events.

This 1821 public document confirms the death of Mr. John Bell.

4.

THE LEGEND: On December 20, 1820, John Bell's life came to an abrupt end soon after the family discovered a suspicious vial of liquid in the house. He was seventy years old. The cause of death? Poison! The suspect? None other than wretched old Kate, who reportedly cackled in triumph when she learned of Mr. Bell's fate. The studio behind a 2006 Bell Witch movie declared this "the only documented case in U.S. history (validated by the State of Tennessee) in which a spirit caused a person's death."

THE TRUTH: In Tennessee in 1820, few seventy-year-olds would have survived any type of serious illness. "As to the 'official statement about his cause of death,' this has been misrepresented by those attempting to make money through movies," says Ms. Reid, the historian. She explains that the state put up a sign in honor of the legend many years ago, but does it officially declare murder-by-ghost? See for yourself on the next page.

THE BELL WITCH TODAY

The legend of the Bell Witch survives partly because many ghost hunters have gotten chills investigating the property where the Bell house used to be—especially the deep cave underneath. They cite unmistakable voices and photographic evidence of ghostly forms. Mr. Bell departed the property almost two hundred years ago, but according to some, the Bell Witch did not.

Might believers be right? It's possible that the sillier chapters in the 1894 book were completely false while others were not. For example, some researchers suggest that the entity now known as the Bell Witch might actually have been Betsy Bell's poltergeist. Poltergeists are a type of "psychic temper tantrum," says Loyd "Professor Paranormal" Auerbach. (See page 45 for more.) Regardless of what happened long ago, the present owner of the Bell Witch Cave has said that many bold thrill-seekers have vowed to spend the night there—and have failed to last more than a few hours. Allegedly, the sound of a wailing woman is what drives them out.

The Tennessee Historical Commission salutes the Bell Witch.

3C 38

BELL WITCH

To the north was the farm of John Bell, an early, prominent settler from North Carolina. According to legend, his family was harried during the early 19th century by the famous Bell Witch. She kept the household in turmoil, assaulted Bell, and drove off Betsy Bell's suitor. Even Andrew Jackson, who came to investigate, retreated to Nashville after his coach wheels stopped mysteriously. Many visitors to the house saw the furniture crash about them and heard her shriek, sing, and curse.

TENNESSEE HISTORICAL COMMISSION

LET US TAKE A MOMENT TO REFLECT

Mirror, Mirror, on the wall . . . who's the foulest specter of them all? Those who grew up in Tennessee might say the Bell Witch. Others are more likely to fear a ghost by the name of Bloody Mary. Both of these wicked wraiths share a common trait: According to folklore, they may be summoned with mirrors. Meeting the Bell Witch commonly requires a child or teen to say, "I believe in the Bell Witch!" three times while looking in a mirror at midnight. In contrast, Bloody Mary doesn't care if you believe in her or not. Either way, she'll get you. Foolish young mortals are usually instructed to turn off the lights and say her name into a bathroom mirror. In some parts of the U.S., she might respond faster to "Bloody Mary, come and get me" or "Bloody Mary, I got your baby." Admittedly, she can get a little picky when it comes to the whole chanting procedure. The only other detail is that you must repeat your chant anywhere from three to thirteen to 100 times—depending on which legend you choose to believe. And who exactly is the lady behind the legend? Most often, she is linked to Queen Mary I of England. From 1553 to 1558, hundreds were executed during her reign.

No longer content to haunt campfires and sleepovers, Bloody Mary has found a new way to tell her story: She got an e-mail account! In recent years, a frightful chain letter has circulated on the Internet. Anybody who receives the e-mail must forward it to fifteen people or suffer the murderous consequences. The person who wrote it claims those were the instructions she received via Instant Message from a little girl whose name rhymes with "Buddy Scary."

HIDE (FROM) YOUR VALUABLES!

Mirrors are not the only household objects to watch out for. In Japan, any item that reaches its one hundredth birthday is said to transform into a type of ghostlike being. This is known as *tsukumogami*, meaning "artifact spirit." Some items simply grow limbs and happy-looking facial features; however, cracks or tears in other items may result in sharp, jagged teeth and menacing eyes. Electronic devices like Game Boys do not become *tsukumogami*. Such spirits are, in a sense, "allergic" to the electricity that otherwise brings so many modern inventions to life. Still, all of this is great news for action-figure collectors! Just don't leave your fully poseable Venom anywhere near your Peter Parker come 2107.

Karakasa

Morinji-no-okama

Chochinobake

Railroad Stories magazine,
June 1933

CHOO-CHOO...BOO!

Vehicle: Steam-powered locomotive
Location: Pittsfield, Massachusetts
Top Speed: Over 100 mph
Specifications: In February of 1958, Mr. John Quirk, owner of the Bridge Lunch diner, informed reporters that he had just witnessed a phantom train chugging underneath North Street bridge. When it appeared again in March, every customer in the diner saw a solid-looking steam engine travel east, along with several coaches and even a baggage car. In both instances, railroad officials couldn't help but point out that no steam engine had operated on that line for years.

GHOSTS ON THE GO

FLY THE NOT-SO-FRIENDLY SKIES.

Vehicle: Lockheed TriStar L-011 jumbo jet
Location: 30,000 feet above Earth
Top Speed: 600 mph
Specifications: Captain Bob Loft met a mucky fate—along with ninety-eight passengers—when Eastern Airlines Flight 401 crashed into the Florida Everglades in 1972. Their lives ended there, the plane's story wasn't over. Some parts of Flight 401 were plucked from the muck and installed in other planes. Crew members aboard Flight 318 reported an apparition identical to Captain Loft. On another flight from New York to Mexico City, five stewardesses and an engineer met a man by the name of Don Repo. Mr. Repo was also an engineer . . . who had perished alongside Captain Loft. "Watch out for fire on this airplane," the late Mr. Repo warned. One of the plane's engines malfunctioned soon after that.

THE TRAFFIC WAS MURDER.

Vehicle: Vauxhall Astra automobile
Location: Burpham, England
Top Speed: 130 mph
Specifications: On the night of December 11, 2002, drivers on the A3 highway claimed to witness a horrible car crash . . . that didn't actually occur on December 11, 2002. Regardless, that was when police responded to multiple eyewitnesses who swore a vehicle had spun into the overgrown brush along the side of the road. Dubiously searching by moonlight, the police found nothing—at first. The next day, they discovered a mangled car—and a five-month-dead corpse—that once belonged to Christopher Chandler, an alleged robber on the run from the law. He had been reported missing in July of 2002.

THE HAUNTED HOUSE ON THE HUDSON

Helen Ackley was standing outside her family's new home in Nyack, New York, when a group of neighborhood kids walked up to her. They were eager to meet Mrs. Ackley for reasons that weren't immediately clear. And yet, when Mrs. Ackley invited them inside for a tour, two of the kids declined.

"They think there's ghosts in there," revealed one girl in the group. "They're scared. Did you know you bought a haunted house?"

No, the Ackley family did not know. But they were about to find out.

It was July of 1967. For several years, the Victorian-style house near the Hudson River had sat empty and in need of repairs. During that period, eyewitnesses began to describe faces gazing down from high-up windows.

"It was considered one of those spooky old houses," remembers Mrs.

Built in 1903, the house in Nyack, New York, belonged to the Ackley family from 1967 until 1993.

A 1971 yearbook photo of Cynthia Kavanagh, who believes she grew up in a haunted house.

Ackley's daughter Cynthia, who spent most of her teen years there. Now living on the other side of the country, Cynthia Kavanagh told ENCYCLOPEDIA HORRIFICA exactly what it was like growing up inside a haunted house: Unidentified voices. A rumbling bed

"AS A MATTER OF LAW, THE HOUSE IS HAUNTED."
—THE NEW YORK STATE SUPREME COURT

Surprisingly, the Ackley family's "Haunted House on the Hudson" is actually more famous among lawyers than among ghost hunters. The above quote can be traced back to a real estate deal gone bad. A man from New York City by the name of Jeffrey Stambovsky was going to buy the Ackley house in 1989 . . . until he learned about the house's supposedly haunted history. He asked for his money back, but Mrs. Ackley said it was too late. Their battle eventually ended

up in an appeals court, where the house, in a sense, was officially declared haunted by the State of New York! Here's the reasoning: When a house is widely perceived to be haunted, the seller of the house is obligated to tell potential buyers. That's because the new owner might not be able to resell it for very much money later on. So, basically, the judge was saying that nobody wants to buy a haunted house. Yes, it's hard to believe, horror fans, but it's true.

that woke her up for school every morning. A hanging lamp that moved by itself. "Like someone was playing with it," she says. "Bobbing back and forth. I saw it myself."

From the beginning, even the bravest of souls were intimidated by the spooky doings. The family's six-foot-tall plumber refused to work past 4:00 P.M. on any given day because he kept hearing footsteps on the stairs. Around the same time, Ms. Kavanagh's father, "never the type of person to get scared easily," insisted that Mrs. Ackley leave on a night-light after bedtime.

"So a big, burly plumber, a stoic dad, and the neighborhood kids all felt something!" Ms. Kavanagh says. Although the good-natured retiree laughs about the house now, one encounter chilled her to the bone. It occurred late at night, when her parents and two younger siblings had already gone to bed. Careful not to wake anybody, she tiptoed into her own bedroom.

"I looked into the room," she says. "And there was a young woman, probably in her twenties. She was sitting on my bed so that I could see her in the mirror on my dresser. She luminesced. She was wearing a white chemise gown and brushing her hair. Brown hair. I couldn't see into the mirror to tell if there was a face, but I knew she wasn't supposed to be there."

What would most teenagers do in such a situation? Scream? Faint? Leap out of a window? Not the levelheaded young Ms. Kavanagh. She apologetically told the apparition, "Don't let me disturb you." Then she calmly distracted herself by watching TV in another room. A half hour later, her bedroom was phantom-free.

Light fixtures inside the house were said to sway without any visible cause.

GIFT-GIVING GHOSTS?

Just before moving out of the Nyack house to go live with her new husband, Ms. Kavanagh discovered a tiny pair of silver tongs on her bed. They were the type of "rather antique-looking" utensil that might be used to serve sugar cubes at a tea party. "I guess the ghost left them," Ms. Kavanagh's sister had said of the mysterious wedding gift. Over the years, the family also received rings and coins.

Once, her sister-in-law, Paula, received a penny, which was promptly tossed in a change jar. "If they don't think I'm worth more than a penny," Paula said, "then I'm insulted." The next week, a whole

dime appeared—except it was useless because it was bent! Although it seems unlikely these items were given by ghosts, nobody in the family has been able to explain them to this day.

The most likely culprit would seem to be Ms. Kavanagh's mother. Until she passed away in 2002, Helen Ackley always seemed to delight in proving to people that her house was haunted. She even published a lengthy eyewitness account in the May 1977 issue of *Reader's Digest*. When asked if her dearly departed mother might have returned to the house to reside there happily ever after (and after), Ms. Kavanagh says, "That's where we're hoping she is."

Q & a

WITH PROFESSOR PARANORMAL

HIS KNOWLEDGE OF THE UNKNOWN WILL ASTOUND YOU.

Loyd "Professor Paranormal" Auerbach lives for the afterlife. As one of the nation's leading experts on ghosts, he has authored many books with long and tantalizing titles, including *ESP, Hauntings and Poltergeists: A Parapsychologist's Handbook* (1986); *Hauntings and Poltergeists: A Ghost Hunter's Guide* (2004); and *A Paranormal Casebook: Ghost Hunting in the New Millennium* (2005). He holds an advanced degree in parapsychology, a field best described as the study of the unexplained.

When ENCYCLOPEDIA HORRIFICA invited the Professor to share his expertise, he kindly took time off from his weird and wonderful work to dine with us at our worldwide headquarters in New York, New York.

EH: How do you define the word "paranormal"?

Loyd Auerbach (LA): The word "paranormal" really means "on the side of normal." So, technically, anything that we can't explain using what we consider normal science should be considered "paranormal."

EH: What exactly is a ghost?

LA: A ghost, in legend, is the spirit of someone who has died, who is around us in some form and capable of interacting with us. [Parapsychologists] use the term "apparition." And that describes our mind surviving the death of the body. An apparition is capable of interacting with us in some way.

EH: What are some perfectly normal phenomena that are often mistaken for ghosts?

LA: Sounds coming from the plumbing. Knockings and things like that. An unusual sound in the house—the house "settling" is a fairly common thing. Reflections of light from cars driving by.... Low-frequency sounds can actually cause you to see things out of the corner of your eye, and sometimes anything from pipes to electronics can create a low frequency. Sounds can make you feel a little bit anxious, too. And we also know that magnetic fields can cause experiences.

EH: What are the most indispensable tools of the ghost hunter's trade?

LA: Interviewing skills. The ability to ask questions and to listen carefully—that is probably the most important tool.

EH: Have you witnessed any cases in which ghosts have actually harmed a living human being?

LA: It's rare that objects move in cases of actual ghosts.... When people get hurt, it's usually because of their response to the ghost—if the person runs away, for example. Other than that, we always say, "Do not duck into the path of a flying object!"

EH: Can anybody communicate with ghosts?

LA: Anybody can communicate with the dead in the sense that we can provide them with communication. The question is: Can we get communication back? So if there was a ghost in this room, I could talk all I want and theoretically the ghost could understand because it is able to pick things up, but could I pick up things from the ghost? There is an openness that's necessary—something in your [mind's] wiring—and some of us are more skilled in that area than others.

Although Professor Auerbach is skeptical toward most ghost photos, he says many in his field believe in old favorites like The Brown Lady of Raynham Hall. "There's a story behind it," he says. "There's no story behind most 'orb' photos." Turn to page 58 to make up your own mind about the Brown Lady's story and today's digital "orb" photos.

"THE BIG THREE"

#1. Apparitions: Personalities that survive the death of the body. Capable of interaction with the living.

#2. Hauntings: Intense emotions or events "recorded" by an environment. They replay over time like a scary DVD stuck on repeat. For example, sobbing noises in a hotel room might be the imprint of a murder that took place in that room long ago.

#3. Poltergeists: Manifestations of living people who are unhappy—sometimes resulting in flying objects and other physical effects. Professor Auerbach says some of the most impressive poltergeist cases involve people who see ghosts of *themselves*.❋

❋ Most ghost hunters feel the makers of the famous 1982 movie *Poltergeist* got it all wrong. Traditionally, a poltergeist—meaning "noisy ghost" in German—has nothing to do with ancient burial grounds or furious interdimensional vortexes.

EH: Do ghosts have a sense of humor?

LA: People have a sense of humor, so people's ghosts have a sense of humor. Two rules I've learned: One—your personality does not significantly change when you die. And two—you don't get any smarter. Dying does not significantly improve your IQ! You don't suddenly open up to the universe and know the secrets of everything. And you don't know the future.

EH: What's the most haunted city in America?

LA: My guess? The most haunted city in the United States would be the most populated city in the United States. That would be this one!

[Ed. note: ENCYCLOPEDIA HORRIFICA has never been more pleased to call New York City its home.]

To Catch A Ghost!

ACTIVATE INFRARED SCANNERS. THE HUNT IS ON.

To catch a ghost, assemble the most level-headed team of people you can find. They must be trustworthy and perceptive....

But that's not all it takes.

To catch a ghost, look each of your team members in the eye and ask, "Are you truly prepared to set foot in a house that might be haunted?" Don't forget to ask yourself that question, too.

To catch a ghost, ask more questions when you arrive at the site of your first investigation: *What type of being does each witness describe? Is it full-bodied and humanlike? Misty and barely there? Has the being ever predicted a future event?*

But to truly catch a ghost—at least, to capture possible evidence of one—your team will require one important item that every professional ghost hunter owns. No, it's not one of the proton pistols from *Ghostbusters*. It is a black suitcase. Because that's the only way you're going to carry all of your really cool hi-tech gear!

Now, even though the equipment looks impressive, that doesn't mean it always works. Many ghost hunters (such as the ones you'll meet on page 49) are quick to point out an important fact: There is no perfect "ghost detection" device because no one knows exactly what ghosts are made of. Or if ghosts even exist at all.

On that last matter, ENCYCLOPEDIA HORRIFICA keeps an open mind. By the end of this chapter, you probably will, too.

Among professional ghost hunters, some enjoy being called ghostbusters. Others do not. The hugely successful movie of the same name is phantasmic fun but pure fiction.

The Original
GHOSTBUSTERS
Starring **Larry Storch**
Forrest Tucker
VOLUME 2

R.I.P.

Continental
Video

See the series that started it all!

Many believe the term *ghostbusters* did not exist before the 1984 movie, but this is untrue. A little-known TV series debuted on Saturday mornings in 1975.

46

THOMAS EDISON: GHOST HUNTER?

"Edison Working on How to Communicate with the Next World" read a headline in the October 1920 issue of *The American Magazine*. Did one of the most famous inventors of all time figure out a way to contact the dead? Probably not. However, Edison did test such a device, according to published reports in the 1920s and 1930s.

THEN

The above ghost-hunting kit belonged to Harry Price, an early pioneer in the field. Mr. Price did chase a few genuinely spooky ghosts. However, he spent more time chasing newspaper headlines . . . even if it meant making up wild stories. In 1932 alone, he announced that he was investigating a talking mongoose (it didn't), and then he set out to transform a German goat into a young man (he failed). Today's ghost-hunting professionals tend to take their work much more seriously. As you'll see on the next page, they have the hardware to prove it.

47

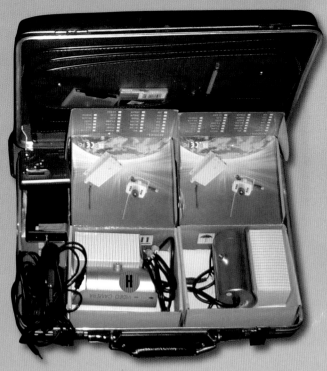

(A) MOTION DETECTOR

Got a big house? Buy a dozen of these. Thirty-six AA batteries not included.

(D) NATURAL EM METER

Measures low-level energy emitted by humans, animals, and . . . others?

(H) INFRARED VIDEO CAMERAS

Waterproof. Transmit images in total darkness. Invest in two for twice the ghoulish fun.

(B) INFRARED THERMOMETER

Locates hot spots. Turns off automatically (in case something happens to you).

(E) DIGITAL THERMOMETER

High accuracy. Measures from -58° F to 1382° F. Enter subzero houses at your own peril.

(C) EMF METER

Identifies electromagnetic, electric, and radio/microwave disturbances. Fast!

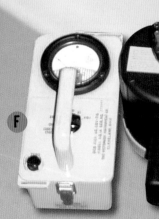

THE COST OF THIS SUITCASE ALONE EQUALS $1,000!

(F) GEIGER COUNTER

If this detects radioactivity, you've got much bigger problems than ghosts.

(G) INFRARED SPOTLIGHT

Candle power: 1 million. *Come out, come out, whatever you are!*

(I) 35MM SLR FILM CAMERA

Includes flash and zoom lens. Capturing a phantom on film can be tricky. See page 62.

(J) DIGITAL CAMCORDER

SONY NightShot Plus recording system. It's not afraid of the dark. Are you?

SPECIAL INVESTIGATION

DUTCHESS COUNTY, NEW YORK——The phone rang late on the last day of August. It was a man by the name of Daniel Sturges, whom everybody calls "Dan." He wanted to make sure ENCYCLOPEDIA HORRIFICA was still interested in observing his work.

"I don't know if you've ever been on an investigation before," he said with some hesitancy, "but...uh...according to the guy who lives there, this place is really active."

Active? People are supposed to be active. Not places.

"It might get a little spooky," Dan added. "He says there's an old lady walking around."

Because Dan is a founding member of a group called Paranormal Investigation of NYC (www.paranormal-nyc.com), it was immediately clear that he wasn't referring to any ordinary old lady. He was talking about the ghost of one. A desperate family needed help, and Dan was determined to provide it.

This is the completely true story of what happened two days later on the first Saturday of September.

2:00 P.M.——The team meets on 207th Street in Manhattan. Dan is a big man, bald and tattooed and upbeat. If he's afraid of what's to come, he doesn't show it. To him and team leader Dominick "Dom" Villella, cramming thousands of dollars of advanced technology into a small automobile is nothing special. It's all in a day's work.

"Sometimes we don't pack everything," says Dan. "But for this mission, we do."

After some rearranging, Dom lifts his head from the trunk and manages to fit everything inside. He's solemn and focused and much shorter than Dan. Surprisingly, he looks more like a science teacher than a brave battler of ghosts. But only at first glance...

When it comes to ghost hunting, first glances can be deceiving.

2:15 P.M.——Our destination is a tiny town about seventy miles from New York City. On the way there, Dom and Dan explain that most of their clients find them via the Internet. In addition to their own Web site, they advertise their services on another site, resulting in about two serious calls or e-mails per week. They list themselves under "Housing Needs."

Along with Jennifer Warfel, an enthusiastic new team member and avid fan of *Buffy the Vampire Slayer*, Dom and Dan recall a few past cases, most of which provided no evidence of the afterlife. For example, one smelly house was found to be "haunted" by nothing more than three residents who simply didn't do enough cleaning! Occasionally, the group does encounter some genuinely strange happenings, though.

"We have a piece of film that appears as though a white mass passes through me, into the room, and disappears into a wall," Dom says of one site in Rock Tavern, New York. "I saw it as it was happening, plus we caught it on video."

In passing they mention a site called the Willowby House. It sounds like the type of place where polite British grandmothers knit by the fire as they enjoy marmalade sandwiches and chamomile tea. It's not. For details, keep reading.

Jennifer, Dom, and Dan prepare to enter the house for the first time.

3:05 P.M.—Working "on-site" can get complicated. With just a few more miles to go, the ghost hunters offer a list of dos and don'ts:

Always keep your eyes on your gear, so that ordinary mistakes aren't recorded as "ghosts." That means no flash photography around the infrared cameras.

Never wander off by yourself. In the event of an apparition, two witnesses are better than one.

THE EIGHT STAGES OF FRIGHT

A good, thorough ghost hunt like the one described in this chapter usually lasts about four hours. Different ghost hunters prefer different methods, but Dom and Dan usually proceed as follows:

Initial Consultation—Witnesses are often interviewed separately. If their stories don't match, this casts some doubt on their claims.

Setup—Hi-tech recording devices are placed in only the darkest and spookiest of locations.

Walk-Around #1—The team explores the site with cameras, atmospheric thermometers, and other gadgets.

Doughnut Break—The team steps out for about an hour in order to see if their equipment picks up any readings when no (living) people are home. Plus, a ghostbuster's gotta eat!

Walk-Around #2—Recording devices are checked for "anomalous" readings during this time.

Ghost Watch—Late at night, the team shuts off all lights and attempts to communicate with the offending spirit. This takes at least fifteen minutes per room—if everybody can control their fear for that long.

Cleansing—If a site is believed to be haunted, the team explains to the ghost that it must leave now. They offer precise instructions in case the ghost is confused about its location.

Final Consultation—The team leader discusses any findings with the client. The client is told how they might continue to make peace with the ghost.

And most important of all, Dom says, "Be careful not to scream, not to frighten the people inside the house. If you feel something even touch you, I know the natural reaction if something touches you is to scream. *Really* try not to."

"Yeah," Dan adds. "Don't freak out in front of the client. That's a biggie."

3:40 P.M.—The team arrives at a 206-year-old house atop a small hill. This is it.

At the front door, they receive a warm welcome from Mrs. Donnelly, a full-time nurse with a bright smile and five kids. It was her husband who first contacted the team. Mr. Donnelly isn't home from work yet, so Dom and Dan take advantage of this opportunity to interview Mrs. Donnelly as she leads everybody up to where the family lives on the second floor.

Although she has witnessed few if any of the incidents described over the phone by her husband, she's seen "orbs," or tiny balls of light, floating all through the house. Her youngest daughter—an energetic middle schooler with long blond hair—has seen one ghost so many times that she gave it a name: George.

"It even came into my bedroom once," she says.

4:10 P.M.—Mrs. Donnelly gives a tour of the house, including the bedrooms. In her own room, she points to the side of the bed

Mrs. Donnelly (on the right) describes the recent happenings in her house.

"where the ghost likes to hang out." She also claims that orbs sometimes cluster around one of the two windows in the corner.

In her fifteen-year-old daughter's room—an oddly shaped space with windows that peer out into a sea of treetops—Mrs. Donnelly speaks of an electric fan that lifted up and smashed against the floor without anybody touching it. Presently, the daughter is living with another relative. So far the only odd noise emanating through these halls is the sound of *The Fairly OddParents* playing on Nickelodeon in the TV room.

During a moment alone, Dom whispers to Dan, "What do you think?"

Dan is unsure.

4:50 P.M.—As a preschooler plays with a plastic fighter jet in the TV room, Dom and Dan munch on nachos and settle upon a strategy. They'll set up a camera downstairs near the front porch, another camera in the hallway, and cameras in two bedrooms.

The team will accept no money for their services tonight, but there are worse fates than getting paid in nachos.

The teen daughter's room.

"So is this just a hobby?" Mrs. Donnelly asks later, over pepperoni pizza.

"Well, it's a little more than a hobby," Dom says after some thought. "Really, it's a quest."

The part that he enjoys most about his work is helping ordinary people solve problems.

6:23 P.M.—Mr. Donnelly finally arrives and shakes everybody's hand.

"I'm tired——and covered in cat pee," he says. "I need a shower."

Not exactly what the team expected to hear!

6:35 P.M.—"I'm human again," Mr. Donnelly says upon his return.

It turns out he installs and cleans carpets for a living, which explains the pet stains. He's been working especially hard lately.

"Did you guys see the photos at all?" he asks as he activates a digital camera.

"That's an unusual thing," Dom says. He squints at one image in the camera's tiny screen. There seem to be two photos of the same place, taken from different angles, in which an orb appears. Since it shows up in the same location both times, it couldn't be a dust particle. Perhaps there was simply something on the lens. . . .

Dom uploads the photos onto his laptop. There, amidst images of the Donnellys' camping trip and a birthday party at Chuck

Dom and Jennifer set up equipment near the front entrance.

E. Cheese's, the team finds a number of orb photos, including several in the master bedroom. Mr. Donnelly took them. Apparently, he doesn't even take a nap in there without keeping the camera at arm's length. He's been on the lookout for weeks——ever since the ghost turned violent.

7:10 P.M.—Mrs. Donnelly and the kids have left to stay elsewhere for the evening.

"Okay," says Dan, who was getting antsy. "Now we begin to have some fun."

The team unpacks suitcases, boxes, and duffel bags. They unspool what seem like miles of electrical cable, connecting four video cameras to a high-powered laptop computer placed in the kitchen. This will be their mini command center for the rest of the evening.

7:45 P.M.—Dom explains to Mr. Donnelly how a Trifield EMF detector works and defines what they're looking for. "Sudden spikes," Dom says. If the needle on the

A window in Mrs. Donnelly's bedroom where orbs have appeared. "I thought they were angels," she said.

HIS NAME IS GEORGE

GHOST STORY!

At approximately 7:00 P.M., Mr. Donnelly shared his story with ENCYCLOPEDIA HORRIFICA. Here, in his own frightened words, is why he felt he had no choice but to call in the professionals:

"Well, this is how it started. I woke up about three o'clock in the morning, and there was a blue ball right in front of my face. I thought maybe it was a dream kind of a thing, but it happened three or four times. I talked to my wife about it, and she said she hadn't seen anything. So one night I took my digital camera, and I got it on film. And that was cool, and I snapped some more photos. It was fun!

Then I started seeing this mist in the house, and out of the mist came a guy. He's very friendly. He waves at the kids. He wasn't hostile or anything like that. And that was all fun and dandy. And then there were the shadows next, and then the footsteps up and down the hallway—all night long. And then the little wooden [toddler] gate we have in the hall just started slamming and slamming and slamming. And then the kids started getting afraid.

And then about three o'clock in the morning, about a month ago, or a month and a half ago, I got pulled out of bed—by my hair. Pulled right up out of bed on the floor. That was pretty scary. My wife woke up. She heard me yelling and screaming. I thought there was somebody in the house at first. You know what I mean? But there was nothing there. . . .

Well, then, nothing happened for a little while. We still had the little balls shooting around. That guy, George—we didn't see him for a while, but we heard him constantly. That's what the kids call him—George.

[My youngest daughter] said he said, 'Hi, my name is George,' and waved at her.

And then I was outside smoking a cigarette one night, and I felt something grab my shoulder. I thought it was a leaf or a branch or something. And when I grabbed it, it moved. And it clenched harder. I looked, and I saw a hand on my shoulder. It was gray. It had long fingernails. I couldn't look past this point to see what it was. And then another hand grabbed the other shoulder, and I couldn't move. I couldn't move at all. I couldn't move my legs. I couldn't move my arms. I couldn't turn around. I couldn't yell. And I couldn't breathe. And it felt like, it felt very malicious in intent. It felt like it wanted to hurt me real bad. It wasn't pleasant—at all. I didn't know what it was, but I didn't like it. It made me feel very vulnerable.

That's why I e-mailed these guys. Because I don't want to play anymore. I don't. The game's over. It's time for it to go."

Mr. Donnelly takes ghost hunter Jennifer Warfel for a tour of his family's front lawn, where much of the activity has occurred. Although summer has not yet ended, it's a cold and windy night.

mirror shoots in one direction or the other, that indicates something odd about the electromagnetic frequency in a particular room. Electromagnetic waves are a lot like the invisible magnetic charge that attracts magnets to a refrigerator, only harder to detect.

Around this time, the landlord stops by. He knows a lot about the house's history. "The wiring is a real mishmash," he says. Dom and Dan will need to keep any electrical problems in mind as they interpret the readings on their equipment.

"We get struck by lightning repeatedly," adds the landlord. "We've had about six fires in this house. One big one since I was here. Another big one before that . . ."

And that's not all: "Did [Mr. Donnelly] mention that one of the deeds actually said that the house was transferred from John Luster, 'lunatic of the first part,' to Jenny Luster?" the landlord asks.

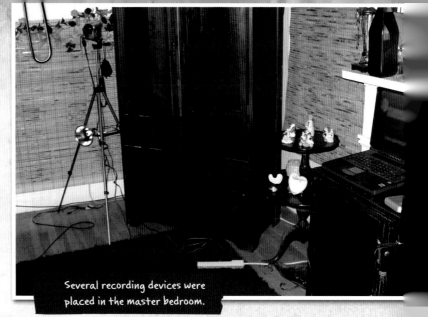

Several recording devices were placed in the master bedroom.

There might have been a murder on the premises, too. Back in 1938. . .

The landlord doesn't stick around long. "Hopefully," he says before leaving, "you won't find anything really unusual—like dead bodies in the walls."

"Well, if you know of any, let us know beforehand!" Dan says.

8:50 P.M.—Time to shut off all of the lights.

All three ghost hunters roam the hallways, letting their gadgets lead the way.

Why does ghost hunting usually happen in the dead of night? Abnormal lights are easier to spot in the dark. Abnormal sounds are easier to hear in the silence.

Dan also explained earlier in the week that their clients are simply more likely to be available after dark, as is Dan. By day, he's an actor and a business owner.

"Plus," he said, "it's just more fun to do it at night, you know?"

9:05 P.M.—While the ghost hunters performed Walk-Around #1, Mr. Donnelly

Closed-circuit cameras record four places at once.

was watching the monitor. He's positive he saw something. "It's not a bug," he says. "You can tell the difference."

Dan and Jennifer tiptoe to the farthest, darkest end of the hallway.

"If there are any spirits here, we'd like to say hello," Dan says.

Not a sound . . . except for the wind pounding against the house. Hard.

The next voice comes from Dan again: "Okay. We're coming back, guys. The squeaky door is us."

9:40 P.M.—We now interrupt this ghost hunt for the Doughnut Break. There's no telling what can happen when a house is left alone to spend some quality time with itself. That's why ghost hunters leave any potentially haunted site for an hour or so. Their clients, too.

So when families are away, do ghosts come out to play? Let's find out! ENCYCLOPEDIA HORRIFICA left its reliable old audio cassette recorder near the Donnellys' front entrance at the bottom of the stairs. And most importantly, we pressed the RECORD button just before exiting the house. Ghost hunters frequently do this in hopes of recording what's known as Electronic Voice Phenomena (EVP). (See inset.)

11:08 P.M.—Mr. Donnelly and the ghost hunters have just reentered the house.

"I got a weird thing at twenty-five minutes," Dan says as he inspects some audio information on the laptop.

Dom takes a closer look. "What would do that?" he asks. "It's the same, exact sound, twice. It might be the wind outside the daughter's window."

11:18 P.M.—Dan returns from an empty

ENCYCLOPEDIA HORRIFICA listened carefully to the forty-five minutes of audio tape we recorded at the Donnelly house. As the timer on the tape recorder ticked off—001, 002, 003—nothing could be heard except the sound of the device itself. At the 375, 406, and 520 markers, knocking and squeaking sounds were heard, but those surely had everything to do with how stormy it was outside. Then came something else entirely: a *thwump-thwump-thwump* noise—like the beating of a heart. Lasting no more than fifteen seconds, it grew louder and louder . . . and then the tape stopped. It would have occurred around 10:27 P.M., well within the time range of other incidents reported by the family. It certainly didn't sound like a human voice. Perhaps it was just the sound of an old tape recorder reaching the end of tape 3, side A.

bedroom. The sound was simply a jiggling window latch. He's sure of it.

Time for another quick walk-around. The team agrees that the equipment has detected nothing suspicious yet. As they peel electrical tape from the floor and pack up different meters, Dom informs Mr. Donnelly that it's quite common for nothing to happen during the early stages of a ghost hunt.

"Sometimes they're active, sometimes they're not," Dom says. The team knows that real-life "ghostbusting" is nothing like the Hollywood version. They never expect to be greeted by flying axes or spinning doll heads like in the movies. Then again . . .

Dom mentions an old stone mansion in

Newburgh, New York. A site that's come up several times now: The Willowby House. Case #1015. Here's how Dom describes it on the team's Web site:

"We were asked to investigate the house for any signs of paranormal activity. What we found surprised all of us. Several times we had readings on our natural EMF detectors. Many times we experienced temperature changes. Gilberto and I while on a ghost watch asked questions and were answered by a woman on four different occasions. . . ."

Speaking of which . . . it's almost time for tonight's Ghost Watch.

MIDNIGHT—What happens during a Ghost Watch? Patience. Surveillance. Long, dreadful moments of quiet confusion . . .

Imagine yourself inside an unfamiliar bedroom painted pitch-black with darkness. The only source of light is the bone-white glow of a two-and-a-half-inch LCD viewfinder. It's attached to a digital night-vision camcorder brought along for the sole purpose of filming ghosts.

Jennifer takes the house's temperature.

If your nerves allow it, join ENCYCLOPEDIA HORRIFICA inside such a room at this very moment as the door shuts behind you. Our only protection against the unknown is two strangers. One of them—an everyday father—believes he was attacked by a ghost while slumbering in this precise location. The other stranger, Dan, spends most of his weekends pursuing unexplained sights and sounds; sometimes he finds them. Right now, he is uttering the following words:

"Is there anybody else in this room? Can you make a sound? Tell us your name. Tell us what year it is. You could knock on the wall. Or touch one of us. . . ."

In an effort to provoke a paranormal response, he even accuses the ghost of being a coward!

Two glowing eyes appear in the window, but it's only the reflection of the camcorder. The room seems darker than ever.

Yes, ENCYCLOPEDIA HORRIFICA may have finally discovered a whole new form of fear. Little did we know that we need only travel to an average bedroom in an average suburban home to—*WHOA! WHAT WAS THAT?!?*

12:18 A.M.—Something terrible happens. Did the ghost dislike being teased? Nobody except Mr. Donnelly will ever know for sure. Just be glad you aren't him.

The only evidence of the "something terrible" is this: At 12:18 A.M., the bed jostles as Mr. Donnelly shouts an unpleasant phrase not publishable in a family-friendly text. Then, he shoots out of the room like a man whose hair is on fire. A troubled man. A man who has just encountered a ghost . . .

At least the bedroom door is finally open. The light returns. It's not enough! Six more hours until daylight . . .

The ghost hunters use infrared light to see things invisible to the naked eye.

Yet, if some parapsychologists are to be believed, stress can also trigger poltergeist activity. Either way, Mr. Donnelly must figure out how to reduce his anxieties, be they paranormal or not.

12:41 A.M.— Dom is informing Mr. Donnelly that nothing in the house will endanger his wife or children. "The house had a completely different feel when they were here," Dom says. "They were happy and energetic. This shields them."

Shields them from what? Dom chooses not to get specific.

"Don't let this drive you crazy," he says. "Learn how to relax yourself, and all of this will disappear."

Later on, when Mr. Donnelly is not in the room, Dom explains why he performed the Cleansing even though he wasn't positive there was a poltergeist. "Either way," he tells Dan and Jennifer, "it sometimes works to either calm the family or actually remove the spirit."

Clearly, both of those goals mean a lot to the team.

ENCYCLOPEDIA HORRIFICA also wishes Mr. Donnelly and his family all the best. Either way. 🖤

12:28 A.M.—Outside, a heavy rain cascades against the window. Inside, the ghost hunters locate Mr. Donnelly curled up on a couch in the TV room. He believes something pressed upon his chest in the darkness of the bedroom. He describes a "black wave."

Dom and Jennifer perform a Cleansing in Mr. Donnelly's bedroom. They tell the ghost, "You no longer belong here. Staying will only cause you sorrow and sadness. Look for the light and join it. The light is your destination, your journey, heaven and paradise. You will find peace in the light."

Despite his actions, Dom is doubtful. Many of the "attacks" described by Mr. Donnelly are perfectly natural symptoms experienced by anybody under a lot of stress.

PHANTOMS ON FILM!

SNAP! FLASH! SH-SH-SHUDDER . . . WHEN GHOSTS POSE, CHILLS DEVELOP.

Some say a picture is worth a thousand words. And pictures of ghosts? Well, the words usually sound like "FAKE!" or "HOAX!" or "DO I LOOK LIKE I WAS BORN YESTERDAY?" But as you'll discover in the chapter ahead, not every ghost photo can be so easily dismissed.

In one startling case, photographer Indre Shira's exact words were "Quick! Quick! There's something!" If his story is true—and ENCYCLOPEDIA HORRIFICA believes it *could* be—Mr. Shira knew he had to act fast when he sighted an "ethereal form" from the Great Beyond. And so his assistant, Captain Provand, captured what eventually became the most famous ghost photo of the twentieth century (pictured).

Sure, this smudge of white may not look like much at first, but who does a ghost need to impress, anyway? Furthermore, no investigation begins and ends with a single photo. In cases such as these, ghost hunters examine the credibility of the photographer(s); they interview other witnesses; they analyze the film negatives (often digital files today); and they research the history of the site where the photo was taken.

Although the image could have been faked quite easily—even before the age of computers—many experts offer but one conclusion: This ghost is no hoax. Seven decades have passed, and during all of that time, nobody has ever proven Mr. Shira or Captain Provand to be untruthful.

The Brown Lady of Raynham Hall was allegedly photographed in Norfolk, England, in September of 1936.

When Indre Shira and Captain Provand first published their ghost photo in *Country Life* magazine, readers were surely shocked. *Country Life* typically featured articles about bird-watching, theater, and a sport called squash. Not the country's *afterlife*.

In the same issue, Mr. Shira also included an eyewitness report. It was long forgotten—until now. On the next page, ENCYCLOPEDIA HORRIFICA proudly presents his original text, as published on December 26, 1936.

THE GHOST OF RAYNHAM HALL
AN ASTONISHING PHOTOGRAPH

A genuine case of spirit photography has yet to be proved, those so far investigated either proving to be fakes or impossible to authenticate owing to the absence of witnesses. Yet the following account and illustration of what happened at Raynham Hall, Norfolk, the seat of the Marquess Townshend, deserves attention, since this particular photograph was taken in the ordinary course of Messrs. Indre Shira's work of photographing Raynham Hall for Lady Townshend, and not under any special circumstances. The case has been investigated by Mr. Harry Price, hon. secretary of the University of London Council for Psychical Investigation, who can give no explanation of the occurrence but refers to a remarkable coincidence in the article on Ghost Photography that follows this account of the Raynham ghost. *

On September 19th, 1936, Captain Provand, the Art Director of Indre Shira, Limited, Court photographers, of 49, Dover Street, Piccadilly, London, W1, and I were taking photographs of Raynham Hall. We commenced shortly after eight o'clock in the morning and had taken a large number of pictures of the house and grounds when, about four o'clock in the afternoon, we came to the oak staircase.

Captain Provand took one photograph of it while I flashed the light. He was focusing again for another exposure; I was standing by his side just behind the camera with the flashlight pistol in my hand, looking directly up the staircase. All at once I detected an ethereal, veiled form coming slowly down the stairs. Rather excitedly I called out sharply: "Quick! Quick! There's something! Are you ready?" "Yes," the photographer replied, and removed the cap from the lens. I pressed the trigger of the flashlight pistol. After the flash, and on closing the shutter, Captain Provand removed the focusing cloth from his head and, turning to me, said: "What's all the excitement about?"

I directed his attention to the staircase and explained that I had distinctly seen a figure there—transparent so that the steps were visible through the ethereal form, but nevertheless very definite and to me perfectly real. He laughed and said I must have *imagined* I had seen a ghost— for there was nothing now to be seen. It may be of interest to record that the flash from the Sasha bulb, which in this instance was used, is equivalent, I understand, to a speed of one-fiftieth part of a second.

After securing several other pictures, we decided to pack up and return to Town. Nearly all the way back we were arguing about the possibility of obtaining a genuine ghost photograph. Captain Provand laid down the law most emphatically by assuring me that as a Court photographer of thirty years' standing, it was quite impossible to obtain an authentic ghost photograph—unless, possibly, in a *séance* room—and in that connection he had had no experience.

I have neither his technical skill nor long years of practical experience as a portraitist, neither am I interested in psychic phenomena; but I maintained that the form of a very refined influence was so real to my eyes that it must have been caught at that psychological moment by the lens of the camera.

"I'll bet you £5," said Captain Provand, with the air of settling the question once and for all time, "that there's nothing unusual on the negative when it is developed."

"And I accept your bet," I replied, shaking hands on the bargain.

When the negatives of Raynham Hall were being developed, I stood beside Captain Provand in the dark-room. One after the other they were placed in the developer. Suddenly Captain Provand exclaimed: "Good Lord! There's something on the staircase negative, after all!" I took one glance, called to him "Hold it, boy!" and dashed downstairs to the chemist, Mr. Benjamin Jones, manager of Blake, Sandford and Blake, whose premises are immediately underneath our studio. I invited Mr. Jones to come upstairs to our dark-room. He came, and saw the negative just as it had been taken from the developer and placed in the adjoining hypo bath. Afterwards, he declared that, had he not seen for himself the negative being fixed, he would not have believed in the genuineness of the picture. Incidentally, Mr. Jones has had considerable experience as an amateur photographer in developing his own plates and films.

Mr. Jones, Captain Provand and I vouch for the fact that the negative has not been retouched in any way. It has been examined critically by a number of experts. No one can account for the appearance of the ghostly figure. But it is there clearly enough—and I am still waiting for payment of that £5!

INDRE SHIRA

NORFOLK LORE

The famous ghost photo on page 58 is believed to feature the Lady Dorothy Walpole (1686–1726) of Norfolk, England. In 1712, Lady Dorothy married Charles "Turnip" Townshend (so named for popularizing the turnip). Alas, some historians believe she picked a bad Turnip. After moving into Raynham Hall, Lady Dorothy revealed that she had once courted another man whom Townshend didn't care for. As a result, she was reportedly locked inside the manor permanently. Confined to just a few stuffy rooms, she eventually died from (a) smallpox, (b) murder, (c) misery, or (d) all of the above. Three centuries later, the details are uncertain, but for Lady Dorothy, the end was merely the beginning....

The Lady Dorothy Walpole's life was filled with heartache. Her death was equally tragic.

EARLY 1800s
A young King George IV, then a prince, spends a night at Raynham Hall. He is soon awakened by a ghastly, pale figure at the end of the bed. He swears, "I will not spend another hour in this accursed house."

1835
According to Ms. Lucia Stone's records at the time, a man by the name of Colonel Loftus encounters a specter with empty, glowing sockets for eyes. The Colonel draws a picture for other guests, who then say they've witnessed it, too.

1836
The ghost reportedly grins at Captain Frederick Marryat in "a diabolical manner." Captain Marryat fires his pistol. The shot passes right through the ghost but ruins a perfectly good wall.

1955
Most books and Web sites state that no ghost has appeared at Raynham Hall since 1936. This may be untrue. In 2003's *Haunted Encounters: Real-life Stories of Supernatural Experiences*, an American tour guide named Docia Schultz Williams describes murmuring voices and other surprise visitations that occurred during her stay.

1926
The 7th Marquess Townshend of Raynham, ten years old at the time, tells his mother that he and one of his friends have seen a ghost on an oak stairwell—the same haunted location that appears in *Country Life* a decade later.

1904
A portrait of Lady Dorothy sells at auction. In the painting (similar to the one above), she wears a brown dress, and, by candlelight, reportedly appears to be missing her eyes. Because of her attire in the portrait—and in many sightings—her ghost is often called the "Brown Lady of Raynham Hall."

WHY DO GHOSTS WEAR CLOTHES?
Like other famous ghosts, the Brown Lady of Raynham Hall is always described as being fully dressed . . . but why? Loyd "Professor Paranormal" Auerbach told ENCYCLOPEDIA HORRIFICA that he wondered the same thing when he was a kid. "Ghosts are energy," he explains. "They're consciousness in our minds, and they communicate with us through our minds, not through our eyes or ears." Therefore, each ghost is transmitting an image of itself *as the ghost sees itself*. As a result, people see ghosts in clothes because ghosts picture themselves in clothes.

SHADOW OF A DOUBT

During the late 1800s and early 1900s, two new phenomena gained in popularity: photography and séances. It didn't take long for greedy swindlers to combine both.

The word *séance* comes from the Old French word meaning "to sit," which is exactly what guests did while their host—the "medium"—attempted to communicate with the dead. As everybody held hands around a table, the medium soon began speaking in strange tongues and gesturing in wild ways. Some mediums then created the illusion of a spectral presence by manipulating elaborate costumes or props. Although photographers were sometimes in attendance, photos of true ghosts were seldom, if ever, taken. The money of guests? Always taken.

HOAX!

During a 1932 séance, the nose of medium Mary M. produced a gob of "ectoplasm," or ghostly energy, containing the likeness of Sir Arthur Conan Doyle.

HOAX!

Illusionist Henri Robin posed for this 1863 photo to prove that anybody with a camera could produce a homemade "ghost."

To the modern eye, most photos from these séances appear silly rather than spooky. Mediums like the one pictured on the left fell out of favor by the 1940s, partly because surveillance technologies were becoming more advanced. For example, shadowy séance rooms once prevented guests from noticing many forms of trickery. Today, night-vision cameras would quickly put an end to such "dispiriting" behavior.

HOW TO VIEW A GHOST PHOTO

Not all fake photos are the handiwork of con artists. Some are simply accidents.

Consider the two "faces" of the S.S. *Watertown*'s doomed crewmen on page 16. They may not have been an intentional hoax, but rather, a coincidental cluster of shadows resembling eyes and noses and well-trimmed mustaches.

Of course, accidental faces—sometimes called "simulacra"—are not the only explanations for these fine, watery fellows, so don't let your hopes evaporate just yet! As with many famous ghost photos, their long-lasting appeal has a lot to do with something you can't see: the trustworthy reputations of the photographer and other witnesses.

That's why ghost hunters must always (1) *look* closely and (2) *listen* closely when examining new photos. Nowadays, those two guidelines are more important than ever. Because digital cameras and image-manipulation software are so common, experts have had to relearn everything there is to know about ghost photos. But even today, the truth could be just a hairbreadth away. . . .

A finger, a smudge, a lock of hair (left), or even a camera strap (right) might later be mistaken for a streak of "ectoplasm" if a photo is taken during the height of fright in an eerie environment.

During the 1990s, photos of so-called "spirit" or "energy" orbs began appearing throughout the world. These are usually tiny objects such as raindrops (pictured) or dust particles reflecting today's powerful camera flashes. At times, digital cameras also tend to omit tiny pixels in some images; these digital "dropouts" can look bright and circular. And other times . . . who can say? Perhaps some orbs are "will-o'-the-wisps"—floating lights described in folklore for centuries.

GHOST OR HOAX?

You're on your way to becoming a true ghost hunter now...right after we put your skills to the test! You didn't think it would be *that* easy, did you?

Some of the images on pages 63 to 65 are famous ghost photos. In the eyes of many researchers, these are actual phantoms caught on film. As for the remaining images, they are hoaxes created by ENCYCLOPEDIA HORRIFICA—strictly for educational purposes. Which are hoaxes and which are ghosts-es? Answers are located on page 137. Happy hunting!

Number 1.
"Old Nanna's Here!"

Number 2.
The Mourning Matron
of Arkham House.

Number 3.
The Ghost of
Freddy Jackson.

(ENHANCEMENT)

Number 4.
The Backseat
Driver.

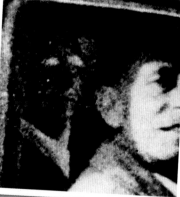

(ENHANCEMENT)

Number 5.
An Ectoplasmic Spiral in
Gorey-Edward Gardens.

Number 6.
The Ghost Girl in the
Burning Building.

(ENHANCEMENT)

ANSWERS ARE LOCATED ON PAGE 137.

THE INVISIBLE CAT

On a chilly autumn night, few cats can resist sneaking into the warm and cozy bed of a human. According to psychic Neva Ankhasha Amenti, ghost cats are no exception.

On October 18, 2005, Ms. Amenti was sound asleep in her guest room at Thayer's Historic Bed 'n' Breakfast in Annandale, Minnesota. Thayer's is a popular home away from home among psychics, ghost hunters, and other professionals who specialize in the unexplained.

"I believe I was the only guest there that night," Ms. Amenti told ENCYCLOPEDIA HORRIFICA. "I went to sleep and the room was closed and locked."

It was around four or five in the morning when she sensed something on her bed and opened her eyes. "I saw little footprints on my bedspread," she explains.

The frisky spirit tiptoed its way from one end of the bed all the way up to her right shoulder. Soon, it was even purring . . . until it abruptly disappeared.

"I just remember laughing," she says. "To see the impression, feel the weight, then to hear the purring all at once, it was very exciting."

Today, Ms. Amenti believes the ghost cat might have chosen her bed because it could sense she was an animal lover with two cats of her own. Surprisingly, both cats, Romeo and Mews, have experienced ghostly

Neva Ankhasha Amenti poses with Romeo, her ghost-fighting feline.

encounters, too. After moving into a new house in Minneapolis, Ms. Amenti discovered them chasing a small brown and white dog that jumped from the furniture and into the floor. And when she says "into the floor," she means right *through* the floor!

Ms. Amenti suspects the dog might have belonged to a previous resident in the century-old house. Romeo and Mews offered no comment, but they continue to stand guard every day.

"FEAR KITTY, KITTY..."

In ancient Egyptian mythology, a protective goddess named Bast was depicted by the image of a fierce lion. Her name meant "female who devours others."

THIS IS *NOT* A GHOST CAT !

Although you are staring Trouble in the face, that's only because this cat happens to be named just that— Trouble. Like the eyes of any other cat, Trouble's eyes turn bright green when a camera flash reflects off of the *tapetum lucidum,* which is a reflective layer behind the retina. The *tapetum lucidum* enables Trouble to see things in the dark that his human owner cannot.

During the Middle Ages, millions of cats were executed in Europe and elsewhere because they were believed by some to have dangerous magical powers.

THIS IS *POSSIBLY* A GHOST CAT !

A man named Alfred Hollidge took this photo in 1974 after he reportedly witnessed his cat, Monet, behaving strangely. On the right is Monet; on the left is . . . something else. Upon developing the film, Mr. Hollidge was perplexed to discover that Monet might have been staring at the dark, animal-shaped entity you see here. The shadowy image was not visible to Mr. Hollidge when the snapshot was taken.

In Assam, India, a phantom tiger was once said to protect graves and other monuments near a tea plantation. Named Bengala, it had all of the same ferocious traits as a living tiger—except it was unkillable.

Oxenby, a British manor house, was once decorated with black shingles arranged in the shape of a cat. And the inside of the house? Not as pretty. It was haunted by a gruesome ghost cat missing one eye and one paw.

MAN'S BEST FIEND

Do you know an omen when you see one? An omen is a warning about a future event: a death, a war, any tragedy big or small. Portents of doom frequently appear as animal ghosts. Among the most famous of animal omens is the Black Dog, an impossibly large hound described by witnesses and storytellers for centuries.

Sometimes headless, always ferocious, Black Dogs have been said to roam in the American South; Scandinavian countries (during Viking days); and many rural and coastal areas of the United Kingdom. Often, the unlucky witness who sees the spectral creature is said to have no more than one year to live. In other tales, the witness has just moments to live . . . because the hound itself is the bringer of death!

Depending on the era and location, Black Dogs have gone by different names. A partial roll call:

Black Shuck of East Anglia

Hairy Jack   Skriker   Padfoot   Mauthe Doog   Capelthwaite

Hateful Thing   Churchyard Beast   Old Shock   Shug Monkey

Galleytrot   Bargheust of Troller's Gill   Gurt Dog   Catalan Dip

Bogey Beast of Lancashire   Guytrash

Swooning Shadow   Cu Sith (usually dark green)

In some places, saying the name out loud is enough to summon danger on four legs. Should this ever happen to you, do not stare at the wretched beast. Turn away. Immediately . . .

Phew—close call!

THE SNARLY YOW OF MARYLAND

Some Black Dog sightings aren't fatal for witnesses; they simply lead to a bad case of the heebie-jeebies. The so-called Snarly Yow allegedly haunts the South Mountain area of Maryland. In recent decades, its snarling form has appeared in the middle of Alternate U.S. Route 40, a roadway in the western part of the state. Drivers have mistakenly believed they ran over a living creature—only to pull over and discover nothing there.

Scorch marks are clearly visible on the north door of Blythburgh Church in Suffolk County, England. Did lightning strike here in August of 1577 . . . or something ___ fiery paws of a Black Dog.

(ENHANCEMENT

THE PHANTOM FERRET OF MIDDLE VILLAGE

Dominick Villella, featured earlier in this book, has witnessed much unexpected weirdness since his team began hunting ghosts in 2003. Among his many missions, the weirdest of all was probably the one involving a stuffed ferret.

By "stuffed ferret," Dominick isn't referring to a cuddly plush plaything you might buy at a zoo's gift shop. No, his story is about a furry dead thing, probably stuffed with sawdust and chemicals.

Here are the facts: In the neighborhood of Middle Village in Queens, New York, a family contacted Dom about apparitions and voices in their apartment. The investigation revealed that their son was possibly being visited by deceased family and friends. In one bedroom, Dom found something else. His Electromagnetic Frequency Detector picked up a signal from a dead ferret that had been stuffed and mounted like a hunter's trophy.

Weirder still, his audio recorder captured the sound of something breathing.

"I used to have a ferret," he says. "And this sounded just like one!"

Nobody knows what, if anything, the ferret was trying to communicate. For now, ENCYCLOPEDIA HORRIFICA suspects the poor creature was advising all pet owners to bury or cremate their dearly departed friends.

Taxidermy is the process of preserving and displaying an animal's body after it has died. While some people regard taxidermy as an art form, many animal lovers regard the process as an act of cruelty. (Would you want *your* body decorating somebody's bookshelf?) With this in mind, a lot of modern taxidermists select only specimens that died in humane ways.

BURIAL PLOT

Whether you're a "cat person" or a "goldfish person," the death of any pet can prove devastating. In 1983's *Pet Sematary*, a dead pet poses all sorts of problems, but they're the type of problems that could be written only by famous fright master Stephen King.

Mr. King's scare-ifying novel tells the story of a dad who places a deceased cat in an ancient, life-giving burial ground. Never mind the fact that a helpful ghost named Victor deliberately warns against this. Sometimes dads just don't listen! Before long, no mere mouse can sate the undead kitty's cravings, and Dad's troubles only get worse from there. It all results in a famous quote stating, in part, "Sometimes dead is better." Quite true, that.

In the real world, evil burial grounds are rare, but pet cemeteries are not. France's *Cimetière des Chiens*, meaning "Cemetery of Dogs," was among the first sites where people could formally say good-bye to their favorite animals. Its oldest graves date back to 1899. Around that same time, a well-regarded veterinarian established the first American pet cemetery, the Hartsdale Pet Cemetery near New York City. Since then, nearly 70,000 beloved creatures have been laid to rest there.

Not one has unburied itself. We think.

Wanna be buried in a "Pet Sematary"? The Ramones didn't! The popular punk-rockers even sang a song about it.

♫ "PET SEMATARY" ♫

Under the arc of a weather-stained board,
Ancient goblins and warlords
Come out of the ground, not making a sound.
The smell of death is all around.

And the night when the cold wind blows,
No one cares, nobody knows.
I don't wanna be buried
In a pet sematary.
I don't want to live my life again.

Follow Victor to the sacred place.
This ain't a dream, I can't escape.
Molars and fangs, the clicking of bones,
Spirits moaning among the tombstones.

And the night, when the moon is bright,
Someone cries, something ain't right.

The moon is full, the air is still.
All of a sudden, I feel a chill.
Victor is grinning, flesh rotting away.
Skeletons dance, I curse this day.

And the night, when the wolves cry out,
Listen close and you can hear me shout,
"I don't wanna be buried
In a pet sematary!"

THE DAY THAT TERROR CAME HOME TO ROOST!

January 1969. The village of Highgate, England. A car breaks down on the side of the road. The driver gets out . . . *and nearly lays an egg when a squawking, half-featherless chicken leaps around in circles, then vanishes!* 'Tis but one of many chapters in a unique ghost story that began in 1626. During an especially cold winter, Sir Francis Bacon was performing an early experiment in meat refrigeration. The key ingredient? One ill-fated chicken. The diabolical bird has allegedly simmered for almost four centuries now, angrily haunting a park called Pond Square. So now you know what to say the next time somebody asks you, "Why did the chicken cross the road?" To get revenge!

Part Three

Behold! The world around you is not the place you thought it was....

Your own neighborhood might contain hidden treasures.

Ordinary people claim to have mastered a "second sight." No eyes required.

Common superstitions are sometimes not as silly as they sound.

And the darkest of secrets await you at your local library.

So leave on your costume. Who cares if the neighbors stare? From now on, the candy spills eternal from the jolly plastic pumpkin, and the Horror Channel is the only channel.

November 1 will never come because...

Every Day Is Halloween

ODD SHOPS & EERIE EATERIES!

SPEND A DAY WITH E.H. AT H.Q. IN N.Y.C.

"Bring me the E.H. Mission Specialist," whispers Joshua Gee from an undisclosed location somewhere in New York City. An impatient man, he taps his headset and wonders, briefly, if he should be alarmed to hear no response....

Suddenly a towering presence appears in the corner of his eye.

"Yes, Chief?" says the Mysterious Mister Grutty, clutching a black, homemade grappling hook—his new favorite thing.

"I'm packing a day kit, Mysterious Mister Grutty, and you'd best do the same. I wish to discover a new secret about the city. Any secret will do, though I would prefer something ghastly."

"Sweet! What will we be needing?"

"An audio cassette recorder, my Albuterol inhaler, and a GPS unit or two. Oh, and one more thing..."

"Yes?"

"Let's not forget the rope this time. Sixty meters. Just in case."

The Mysterious Mister Grutty doesn't respond. He only smiles.

"Aces," murmurs Investigator Gee to no one in particular. As he gazes at a map of Manhattan, he ponders the countless options for this lazy afternoon in the city. "The START button has been pressed, and the game is on. The game is on...."

Today, Joshua Gee and the Mysterious Mister Grutty have decided to pursue a new hobby. It's called geocaching, and it can uncover many secrets in their city as well as yours. Geocaching is best described as a treasure hunt requiring an electronic device instead of a shovel. How does it work? Using handheld Global Positioning System (GPS) receivers, any weekend explorer can search for a hidden waterproof container called a "cache," which usually has a log sheet or even a tiny item inside. With the aid of (1) his Garmin eTrex GPS device and (2) his quick-witted associate, Investigator Gee hopes to find a cache today, so he may triumphantly add his signature to the list of Manhattan's treasure hunters. The cost of a basic GPS device? Roughly $100. The cost of a quick-witted associate? Priceless.

The geographical coordinates for thousands of caches may be found at www.geocaching.com.

I.Q.

N 40° 43.440
W 073° 59.934

N 40° 44.018
W 074° 00.113

CACHE FOUND! Spent day in Park. Learned its (ghastly!) history. Time to feed... —JG

WE'D LIKE TO HAVE YOU FOR DINNER

After a long afternoon of skulking, deducing, and theorizing, the
E.H. team often chooses to unwind at one of the 20,000 diverse
restaurants in New York City. What's on the menu this evening?
A scrumptious case of the jitters, extremely well chilled.

TODAY'S SPECIAL!

2 PERSONALITIES FOR THE PRICE OF 1

In midtown Manhattan—just a short crawl from Central Park—**the** Jekyll & Hyde Club boasts four stories of fright. It's named after Dr. Henry Jekyll and Mr. Edward Hyde, the mad scientist and his even madder alter ego from Robert Louis Stevenson's *The Strange Case of Dr. Jekyll and Mr. Hyde*. Don't be surprised if you find yourself mingling with costumed characters who seem just as maniacal as anything in the book. Truly, every day feels like Halloween at this eeriest of eateries and also at their aptly named Web site (www.eerie.com).

Many locations near Washington Square Park are said to be haunted. It might have something to do with the fact that it was once a site where criminals were executed! Nowadays, you can get a really cheap hot dog there and watch a performance for free.

The Bridge Café near South Street Seaport dates back to 1794. So do the pirate ghosts outside the café who stroll by its windows, according to some customers.

Want flies with that order? Save plenty of room for what's to come next.

ONE SKULL...

As the sun dips behind the skyscrapers, it's nearly closing time at **The Evolution Store** (www.evolutionnyc.com). Hurry up or else you'll have to last a whole night without important staples like resin-coated bugs ($3), genuine skunk skulls ($22), dearly departed scorpions ($29), and ultra-realistic megalodon shark tooth replicas ($45).

The knowledgeable staff at Evolution will also be happy to assist you with all of your *gift-giving* needs. Does a special aunt have a birthday coming up?

OR TWO?

Imagine the indescribable look on her face if she were to unwrap a handsomely framed tarantula! For only $69, it's so much more personal than a Hallmark card.

And if you're in the market for something less dead, why not invest in a miniature two-headed skeleton ($695)? He's not real, but your family members don't need to know that. He would make a lovely centerpiece on any kitchen table. Both of him.

Store manager Alex Minott shows off three gallons of dead flies. Wouldn't you be proud, too?

MAESTRO of PUPPETS

Erik Sanko knows exactly how to pose for a photo in ENCYCLOPEDIA HORRIFICA. Bravo!

"There's no way of duplicating the experience of standing in a room with a little man," says marionette maker Erik Sanko. And what could possibly be better? Standing before an entire stage full of little men!

The stars of *The Fortune Teller* don't ask for much when it comes to pay raises or applause, but they do demand your attention with their lively wooden ways. In Mr. Sanko's show, each is summoned to the opulent residence of the late Nathaniel Ax. There, they encounter a delightfully wicked fortune teller, and instead of an inheritance, each of the flawed characters gets exactly what's coming to him.

Although it takes many weeks to create the mini masterpieces you see here, Mr. Sanko says anyone can become a puppet maker.

"Marionettes are probably the most annoying and complicated to make," says Mr. Sanko. "But a kid could make one out of a paper bag. Out of anything. It just requires a good imagination. And a kid!"

Mr. Sanko is also lead singer of the band Skeleton Key. He co-created the music for *The Fortune Teller* with the same man who gifted the world with the soundtracks to *The Nightmare Before Christmas* and *Corpse Bride*.

What's on the Other Side?

On the other side of this simulated flash card, you'll find one of five symbols: a plus sign, three wavy lines, a square, a star, or a circle. Can you psychically predict which one it will be?

ZENER CARD #1

Amazing Brain Waves!

DOES YOUR BRAIN HAVE HIDDEN POWERS? HOLD THAT THOUGHT.

You probably think you're too old to play with dolls. If so, you're not playing with them properly.

The snapshot on the right was taken by The Society for Research on Rapport and Telekinesis (SORRAT). Just like Yoda in the *Star Wars* saga, the SORRAT group believed they could move objects by focusing the power of their minds in startling new ways.

The photo below was first published by Danish photographer Sven Turck in 1945. Mr. Turck also published photos of a flying chair and even a man who appeared to be spinning across the room like a fastball. The photographer's psychic friends claimed to use a "binding of thoughts" to achieve liftoff.

Could Mr. Turck's leaping table be a hoax? Certainly. But if so, creating such a convincing hoax couldn't have been easy. Back then, there were no digital toolboxes just a mouse click away, so Mr. Turck and his accomplices must have "put their heads together," truly.

TELEKINESIS—the ability to move or deform objects without touching them. Also called "psychokinesis."

A gravity-defying doll?

A leaping table?

ZENER CARD #1

SPECIAL INVESTIGATION

MISSION: To uncover the truth about a top-secret government research program

IN SEARCH OF: An ex-spy willing to tell all

LOCATION: The mailroom

MEMO TO HEADQUARTERS: Star Gate, Grill Flame, Sun Streak, and Phoenix may sound like characters from an *X-Men* movie, but they're not. Keep an "open mind" toward this one.

NEW YORK CITY—It appeared to be an ordinary white envelope. Just another boring letter from the bill collectors at Skulls Unlimited, perhaps. Upon closer inspection, the back was sealed shut by a strip of brown paper to protect its contents from curious eyes. The return address read "Central Intelligence Agency" in Washington, DC....

The super-secret spy agency known as the CIA.

They were responding to ENCYCLOPEDIA HORRIFICA's request for details about a government operation that was off the record until just a few years ago. It was known as Project Star Gate (among other codenames). For over two decades, various government officers were tested for the ability to find things in faraway places—using only the power of their minds! Usually, their orders were to close their eyes and concentrate on a set of geographic coordinates. The most talented agents were recruited to participate in regular sessions for months or even years at a time.

You probably don't believe a word of this. Neither did we. Until we opened the CIA's letter, which you can read for yourself on the right.

But what other proof exists? Might there be a psychic spy willing to go "on the record" with ENCYCLOPEDIA HORRIFICA? You needn't read minds to find out. Simply turn the page....

X-powers: Maybe more real than you thought.

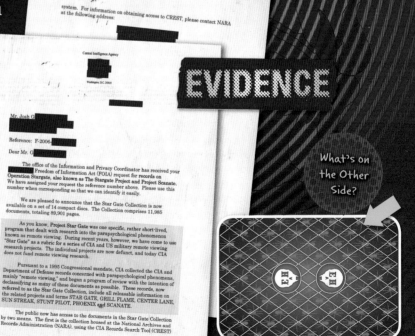

EVIDENCE

system. For information on obtaining access to CREST, please contact NARA at the following address:

Central Intelligence Agency

Washington, D.C. 20505

Mr. Josh G▒

Reference: F-2006-▒

Dear Mr. G▒

The office of the Information and Privacy Coordinator has received your Freedom of Information Act (FOIA) request for records on Operation Stargate, also known as The Stargate Project and Project Scanate. We have assigned your request the reference number above. Please use this number when corresponding so that we can identify it easily.

We are pleased to announce that the Star Gate Collection is now available on a set of 14 compact discs. The Collection comprises 11,985 documents, totaling 89,901 pages.

As you know, Project Star Gate was one specific, rather short-lived, program that dealt with research into the parapsychological phenomenon known as remote viewing. During recent years, however, we have come to use "Star Gate" as a rubric for a series of CIA and US military remote viewing research projects. The individual projects are now defunct, and today CIA does not fund remote viewing research.

Pursuant to a 1995 Congressional mandate, CIA collected the CIA and Department of Defense records concerned with parapsychological phenomena, mainly "remote viewing," and began a program of review with the intention of declassifying as many of these documents as possible. These records, now referred to as the Star Gate Collection, include all releasable information on the related projects and terms STAR GATE, GRILL FLAME, CENTER LANE, SUN STREAK, STUNT PILOT, PHOENIX and SCANATE.

The public now has access to the documents in the Star Gate Collection by two means. The first is the collection housed at the National Archives and Records Administration (NARA), using the CIA Records Search Tool (CREST)

Central Intelligence Agency
Information And Privacy Coordinator
Washington, DC 20505

NO VA 22▒
17 JUL 2006 PM 4▒

MR. JOSH G▒

10009▒▒▒800

What's on the Other Side?

ZENER CARD #2

Q & a WITH A PSYCHIC SPY

WHAT IS THE MATRIX? FIND OUT HERE.

"Here's a really big secret," says former government employee Paul H. Smith (pictured). "Research seems to show that *everyone* is psychic. Most folks just haven't learned yet how to use this ability. But work done at the Star Gate program showed that it could be taught."

From 1983 until 1990, Mr. Smith woke up for work, got dressed, and reported for duty at Star Gate headquarters. There he would check the daily schedule and await his turn to serve his country in a most unusual way. Mr. Smith was what researchers call a "remote viewer." Most often, his job required him to find secret enemy locations in his mind's eye....

And sometimes he turned out to be right.

"The funny thing was how being psychic became just like any other job," says Mr. Smith, author of *Reading the Enemy's Mind: Inside Star Gate, America's Psychic Espionage Program* (2005).

Mr. Smith parted ways with the program in 1990 when duty called in the Mideast. Project Star Gate ended five years after that, but Mr. Smith—and numerous others—exited the program with enough mind-boggling memories to last a lifetime.

REMOTE VIEWING—the ability to see objects or events without looking at them. Also called "clairvoyance."

Project Star Gate began here at Fort Meade, Maryland.

EH: What are some theories explaining how remote viewing is possible? Is it true that *THE MATRIX* is more than a sci-fi movie?

PHS: No, *The Matrix* is just a science fiction movie . . . but many of the ideas in it are real or, at least, could one day become real! For example, a basic remote viewing method called controlled remote viewing (CRV) used the word "matrix" many years before the movie was even filmed. In CRV, the matrix is the source of all information, kind of like how the central computer in the movie is the source of all the information creating the beliefs of the people in the movie's "matrix."

The remote viewer's mind interacts with the matrix to extract the desired information about whatever target is being sought. "But what is the matrix?" you may ask. Well, some of us remote viewers think it has to do with a physics principle called "entanglement." Entanglement is much too complicated to explain here, but some scientists think that through entanglement everything in the universe is interconnected in some way. If that is the case, it may be possible for human minds to "grab" information from other, distant parts of the universe—from the far side of the planet Earth opposite where the remote viewer is, for example.

EH: What types of psychic abilities has the government researched?

Paul H. Smith (PHS): When the Star Gate program began under [research scientist] Dr. Harold Puthoff in 1972, the CIA was more interested in psychokinesis (PK). Using the power of the mind to crash enemy computers or missiles could have been very handy. Unfortunately, they found that PK was very hard to make happen when and how they wanted it to. Since it was too unreliable, and since remote viewing turned out to be more dependable, they decided to focus on that. But they also looked into other things, such as telepathy (so-called "mind reading"), psychic healing, and so on. These other things were interesting, but also less dependable than remote viewing.

The Matrix's Neo vs. Agent Smith: "I've even heard rumors that the movie's screenwriters knew about remote viewing theory," says the *real* "Agent Smith."

What's on the Other Side?

Q&A WITH A PSYCHIC SPY

EH: Could you describe a case in which even you were blown away by your abilities?

> **PRECOGNITION—the ability to predict the future.**

PHS: My most mind-blowing remote viewing session happened on Friday, May 15, 1987. The [assignment] went something like this: "Describe the most important thing for the U.S. government to know about in the next few days."

My impressions were of a warship sailing at night through a sea surrounded by flat sandy shores a long ways off. Then I got the feeling that an aircraft flying some distance from the ship fired missiles at it, hitting it and setting it on fire. There were many more details that I won't go into here. I spent about an hour describing all the strange events I was perceiving in my mind's eye. Finally, my [supervisor] got bored. "You're off," he told me—meaning that he thought I wasn't describing anything real. He had

expected something else, and this wasn't it. The technique didn't work every time, so we were used to getting things wrong from time to time. I stuffed the paperwork from the session in a file folder, and at the end of the day we all went to our homes for the weekend.

Then, around eight o'clock Monday morning I got a call from the operations officer.

"Paul, where's that session you did Friday?" he asked.

"I put it in my file drawer," I said. "Why does it matter? I was off, wasn't I?"

He told me to go look at the morning's paper. There, on the front page, was a major news story: An Iraqi jet fighter had launched two missiles at an American warship, setting it on fire, seriously damaging it, and killing 37 sailors. The event I had psychically described had actually happened—50 hours after I had described it! I have never forgotten that session— it was probably the most remarkable remote viewing experience I've ever had.

The USS *Stark* on fire and . . .

Smith's drawing of what he saw in his mind's eye.

ZENER CARD #3

EH: Were you aware of your psychic abilities prior to joining Project Star Gate?

PHS: Before I was asked by the U.S. Army to become a remote viewer, I had no idea that I was "psychic" in any way. I read science-fiction books about extrasensory perception (ESP) and thought it was really cool. But in junior high, I helped out with a school science fair project that tested for ESP. We tried very hard, but neither my friends nor I showed any ESP ability at all. I came to doubt that ESP was real. Then, many years later, I was asked to become a remote viewer. I thought it might be worth one more try. On my very first try, I once again failed to describe the target. However, I did get strong impressions of a place I'd never been. It turned out to be the shop where the people helping with the experiment stopped afterwards to buy doughnuts. I knew that I had a long way to go in learning how to control my newfound ESP ability. But I also knew that it really did work!

EH: When asked about a secret subject, people sometimes joke, "If I told you, then I'd have to kill you." Do spies ever say that in real life?

PHS: Yes, we often do say that in real life—but it is always meant as a joke. One of the earliest times I remember hearing it was when I asked my friend Tom McNear what sort of intelligence work he did. Tom, I later learned, was a remote viewer. Tom gave me that famous line, "If I told you, I'd have to kill you!" but he was grinning when he said it. A few weeks later it was Tom who told me about remote viewing, once I had signed a promise not to tell anyone else about it. And he didn't kill me!

DST-1810S-387-75
September 1975

DST-1810S-387-75

Preface
Summary

PART I   EXTRASENS
    SECTION 1
    SECTION
    SECTION
        Part
        Part
    SECTION
        Par
        Par
PART II PSYCH
PART III PSYCH
PART IV OUT-
    SECT
    SECT
PART V   CO
PART VI TR
PART VII CA
APPENDIX -

DEFENSE INTELLIGENCE AGENCY

SOVIET AND CZECHOSLOVAKIAN PARAPSYCHOLOGY RESEARCH (U)

SOVIET UNION

PREPARED BY U. S. ARMY
MEDICAL INTELLIGENCE AND
INFORMATION AGENCY,
OFFICE OF THE SURGEON GENERAL

"I have been unable to find any evidence that anyone in the government has started any new remote viewing programs," says Mr. Smith. However, other countries did research such phenomena in the past.

UNCLASSIFIED

PROVIDING CONCRETE IDEAS FOR THE PLANNED INSTITUTE.
THE OFFICIALS SAID DISCOVERIES MADE AT THE
TO BE APPLIED IN A VARIETY OF
AUDIO-VISUAL

UNCLASSIFIED

PAGE:0002

PAGE:0001

INQUIRE=DOC21D
ITEM NO=00014063
ENVELOPE
CDSN = LGX893   MCN = 93030/16139   TOR = 930501051
RATUZYUV RUESDJA3923 0501039-UUAA--RUEALGX.
ZNR UUUAA ZYH
HEADER
R 191039Z FEB 93
FM FBIS OKINAWA JA
TO AIG 4583
RUCWAAA/FBIS RESTON VA//ECON//
RUCWAAA/FBIS RESTON VA//POLCH//
ACCT FBOW-EWDK
BT
CONTROLS
UNCLAS 4A

SERIAL: OW1902103993

BODY
COUNTRY: JAPAN
SUBJ: MINISTRY TO STUDY PSYCHIC POWERS, UFO'S FOR FUTURE INDUSTRY

SOURCE: TOKYO KYODO IN ENGLISH 0935 GMT 19 FEB 93
TEXT:

. ((TEXT)) TOKYO, FEB. 19 KYODO -- JAPAN'S BUREAUCRATS ARE
BEGINNING TO TAKE THE BURGEONING NEW AGE INDUSTRIES SERIOUSLY WITH A
PLAN TO STUDY SUPERNATURAL PHENOMENA, INCLUDING PSYCHIC POWERS AND
EVEN UNIDENTIFIED FLYING OBJECTS (UFOS), GOVERNMENT OFFICIALS SAID
FRIDAY.
    THE MINISTRY OF INTERNATIONAL TRADE AND INDUSTRY (MITI) OFFICIALS
SAID THE MINISTRY PLANS TO FORM A RESEARCH INSTITUTE FOR SCIENTIFIC
STUDY OF ART, CULTURE, AND PARAPSYCHOLOGY -- SUCH AS TELEPATHY AND
CLAIRVOYANCE -- FOR APPLICATION TO NEXT-GENERATION INDUSTRY.
    THE PROPOSED INSTITUTE, WHICH WILL LIKELY BE SET UP IN 1995, IS
THE BRAINCHILD OF A MITI PANEL ESTABLISHED LAST NOVEMBER TO STUDY
CREATION OF AN INDUSTRY MORE SENSITIVE TO HUMAN NEEDS FOR ART, INNER
PEACE, AND OTHER INTANGIBLE THINGS.
    THE OFFICIALS SAID THE PANEL, COMPRISING KEY FIGURES FROM A
VARIETY OF BUSINESS AND CULTURAL CIRCLES, IS ACCUMULATING DATA ON
THE EFFECT OF CULTURAL ACTIVITIES SUCH AS TEA CEREMONIES AND FLOWER
ARRANGING ON THE STATE OF THE MIND THROUGH BRAIN WAVE CHECKS AND
OTHER SCIENTIFIC EXAMINATIONS.
    THE SCIENTIFIC APPROACH WILL ALSO BE TRIED WITH TELEPATHY, UFOS,
AND OTHER PARAPSYCHOLOGICAL AND OCCULT PHENOMENA, LONG IGNORED BUT
GAINING CREDIBILITY OF LATE IN THE SCIENTIFIC COMMUNITY.
    THE RESEARCH WOULD INCLUDE BRAIN WAVE CHECKS ON THOSE WHO CLAIM
TO EXPERIENCE TELEPATHY OR STUDY OF SUCH PHENOMENA AS SOOTHING MUSIC
TRIGGERING QUICKER GROWTH OF PLANTS.
    THE PANEL WILL DRAFT AN INTERIM REPORT ON ITS ACTIVITIES BY MAY

UNCLASSIFIED

Approved for Release
Date   1991

19

JAPAN

What's on the Other Side?

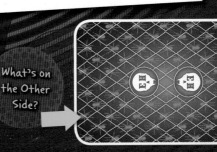

ZENER CARD #4

85

EH: How does your thirteen-year-old son feel about your history as a psychic spy?

EH: Have you ever tried using your psychic abilites to win the lottery?

PHS: Surprisingly, he doesn't seem to think about it very often. I know he doesn't often tell his friends much about me and what I do (though most of his closest friends already know something about it — they've seen me on TV or seen my book). He says, though, that if the topic ever came up in school he wouldn't be shy to talk about it. In fact, in fifth grade he did a science fair project involving remote viewing — and it was successful! His project was selected to be a runner-up in the school district competition.

PHS: As a graduation exercise, I have all my students try to choose the right numbers for the Texas Pick-3 lottery. Once we were only one digit off. (In other words, if the correct numbers were 673, we got 573!). Another time, we narrowed it down to two numbers we had to decide between. We bet on one, and it turned out to be the other. It isn't easy. People often have the wrong idea about ESP. They think it should be simple to get numbers. But because of certain features of the human mind and brain, numbers are really one of the hardest things for ESP to get. But we keep coming closer, and I'm confident we will win one of these days — maybe even the next time we try!

CAN PEOPLE PERFORM E.S.P.?

HYPOTHESIS:

What is "Remote Viewing"?

PROCEDURES

MATERIALS

SOURCES

SESSIONS BY VIEWERS WITH ADVANCED TRAINING

DATA BOOK: ALL SESSIONS

CONCLUSION

"After we were done with all the sessions," says Mr. Smith's son, Will, "we compared the word descriptions and sketches to see if the people who had been taught remote viewing did better than the beginners. And they did."

EH: And, finally, is "Smith" your real name? It sounds a lot like an alias.

PHS: Sorry. If I told you, I'd have to...well, you know the rest! **EH**

BRAIN GAMES

The Sony PlayStation 3: a modern marvel of button-mashing elegance!

Indeed, a 60-gig console with motion-sensitive Bluetooth controllers might already sound perfect, but what if you could upgrade your system to a Sony "PsychicStation"? For several years in Japan, the idea almost seemed possible.

Beginning in late 1991, researcher Yoichiro Sako led the Sony Corporation's covert Project ESPER (ExtraSensory Perception and Excitation Research). Among other paranormal pursuits, Mr. Sako tested several Japanese kids for the same seeing-without-eyes ability described earlier in this chapter.

Published reports have linked the existence of Project ESPER to Sony cofounder Masaru Ibuka because Mr. Ibuka was said to be a fan of the unexplained. However, many believe that Sony also hoped to someday engineer a hi-tech product involving ESP.

When Mr. Ibuka passed away in 1997, Sony announced that it was shutting down the lab, which shocked no one. Far more shocking was their official statement in the *South China Morning Post* on July 7, 1998. "We found out experimentally that yes, ESP exists," said spokesperson Masanobu Sakaguchi, "but that any practical application of this knowledge is not likely in the foreseeable future."

Telekinesis in PS3's *Sonic the Hedgehog*.

What's on the Other Side?

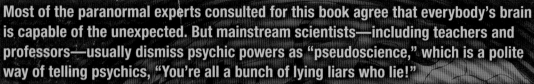

Most of the paranormal experts consulted for this book agree that everybody's brain is capable of the unexpected. But mainstream scientists—including teachers and professors—usually dismiss psychic powers as "pseudoscience," which is a polite way of telling psychics, "You're all a bunch of lying liars who lie!"

Are you a believer or a skeptic? Before you decide, put your own talents to the test. And if you don't observe instant results, remember that paranormal experts agree on one other thing: Psychic powers take practice.

TELEPATHY—the ability to communicate between two minds without using words or gestures.

1. Create twenty-five Zener flash cards* using the template on the right. Photocopy the page and cut out every card, or draw the same set of symbols on small index cards.

2. Ask a licensed parapsychologist to shuffle the deck of cards. Asking a friend will work, too.

3. Sit at opposite ends of a table. Beware of any mirrors or other reflective surfaces that might accidentally reveal what's on the cards. Now, your friend must cup the deck of cards in his or her hands and focus on the symbol that appears on the bottom card.

4. When your friend says to begin, close your eyes. Concentrate very hard. Try to visualize your friend's point of view. What do you see? Can you make out which symbol your friend selected?

5. Keeping your eyes closed so that your friend's facial expressions do not reveal anything, say what you see. Your friend may tell you if you're correct.

6. Record the results and repeat twenty-four more times. Out of twenty-five tries, expect an average of five correct guesses. (That's probably not mind reading. It's statistical mathematics.) And if you got fifteen or even twenty "hits" ... well, those are some truly amazing brain waves.

Many believe that telepathy is common among twins.

ZENER CARD #5   ✻ Dr. J. B. Rhine (1895–1980), a pioneer in ESP research, named the cards after his colleague Karl Zener.

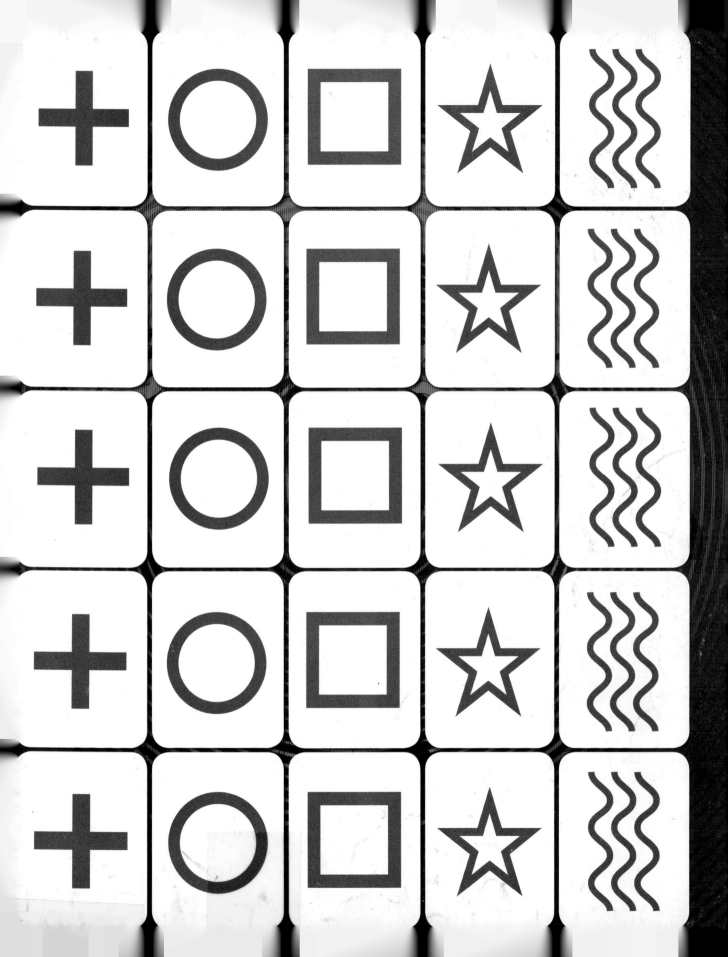

THE BLACK CAT's PATH!

FRIGHT MAKES MIGHT.

Fearology—the study of fear. It's not a real word, but it should be. In fact, from now on, let's agree that it will be. And if you wish to become the world's first fearologist, you don't require any special degrees. You probably already know more than you'd like to know. After all, there are oh-so-many ways to be afraid.

Very often, fear is given a face. That face has come to be known as the mighty Bogeyman, but he goes by many other names and, over time, he has worn many different guises.

In some cultures today, fear is given a medical term. Intense fears toward specific things are called phobias. They are usually a result of terrible experiences in a person's past. For example, if you were to accidentally fall into a deep well filled entirely with underfed toads, then you should expect to develop a severe case of bufonophobia, the fear of toads. Probably for many years to come. But only if you survive, obviously.

Fear is sometimes linked to an unlikely set of popular beliefs. That's called superstition. "Never break a mirror," superstitious types will tell you, "and plan on seven years' bad luck if you do!" Such rules help us feel safer amidst the unpredictable chaos of the daily world.

Then again...does anybody truly want to live a safe and unpredictable life during every moment of every day? No, not us. Not the fearologists. Not even for one chapter.

A nineteenth-century paper cutout toy featuring Monsieur and Madame Croquemitaine ("Mr. and Mrs. Mitten-Biter"), the French Bogeyman and his wife.

Another type of Bogeyman character is the murderous puppet Mr. Punch, featured in British "Punch and Judy" shows since the 1600s.

Every year in New Mexico, performers set fire to a toothless, forty-nine-foot Bogeyman for good luck. His name is Zozobra.

The Bogeymen of today are often movie villains like Freddy Krueger from *A Nightmare on Elm Street*, Parts I through VII.

The fear of big words is called "Hippopotomonstrosesquippedaliophobia." Turn to page 93 for more phobias.

TRUE SUPERSTITIONS

When ENCYCLOPEDIA HORRIFICA said "send us your superstitions," two states took top honors. Our condolences!

"All my life I have heard superstitions and old wives' tales such as never walk under a ladder or let a black cat cross your path. But I was a teenager when I heard the most unusual superstition of all. I had gone to my grandmother's house on some errand. When I got there, my grandmother was running through the house going crazy, chasing a bird. I asked my grandmother what was wrong. She didn't take the time to answer me until she had run the bird out of the house. She then explained that when a bird flies into your house, there will be a death in the family. I laughed, thinking that was the silliest thing I had ever heard. A few days later, my grandfather was outside on a swing. He was holding a shotgun and showing it to my brother. My brother got up off the swing and walked into the house. My grandfather stood up using the shotgun as a crutch, but then the swing hit the trigger. Grandfather didn't survive the accident. I am now a firm believer in superstitions and old wives' tales."

—Theresa Pegelow,
Salisbury, Missouri

"When we were young, we always believed if you step on a crack on the sidewalk, you will break your mommy's back. If you drop a robin's egg and crack it, you will have seven years' bad luck. Or if someone is sweeping the floor and that person sweeps over your feet, you must throw salt over your shoulder or you will have bad luck."

—Dimple Robinson,
Huntsville, Missouri

"My husband has a phobia about Friday the 13th and won't go out on that date. It started when he was eleven years old. He was nervous about the date, so he put a bunch of lucky charms in his pocket and went to school. The minute he got to class, he sat down and the entire back side of his pants ripped due to all of the lucky charms in his pocket! As he got older, any time he had a run-in with the police for a traffic ticket, it happened on Friday the 13th. Another time, he told an old girlfriend that he wouldn't go out on Friday the 13th, but she convinced him to. They were going to go to an outdoor event in Central Park. My husband's restaurant had set up a booth there to sell food that night. They left the house and discovered the car had been towed. When they finally got to the event, out of nowhere a thunder-and-lightning storm came through. On the way home, his girlfriend slipped in the mud and broke her ankle. Coincidence?"

—Michele Lynn, Piermont, New York

"Well, many years ago, I worked as a nurse's aid in a nursing home. First of all, almost nothing is spookier than being in a nursing home at night, especially the one I worked in. That is the first place I ever heard anyone say that deaths always happen in threes. The first death I experienced there was very hard to take. You become very close to these perfect strangers when you take care of them day after day. Everyone would say there would be another death to come soon, and sure enough, you would see the pattern happen. There never was a long time between the deaths; it always happened within a three-month span. . . . When someone dies, I still hear people ask, 'Who will be next?' They always seem to witness the pattern, and this is widely heard of in my hometown area."

—Shonelle Best, Clifton Hill, Missouri

FEAR OF . . .

Accidents: **Dystychiphobia**
Air: **Anemophobia**
Air swallowing: **Aerophobia**
Airsickness: **Aeronausiphobia**
Amnesia: **Amnesiphobia**
Anger: **Angrophobia**
Animal skins/fur: **Doraphobia**
Animals: **Zoophobia**
Ants: **Myrmecophobia**
Automobiles: **Motorphobia**
Bacteria: **Bacteriophobia**
Bald people: **Peladophobia**
Beards: **Pogonophobia**
Beds/bedtime: **Clinophobia**
Bees: **Melissophobia**
Bicycles: **Cyclophobia**
Birds: **Ornithophobia**
Black (the color): **Melanophobia**
Blood: **Hemophobia**
Body odors: **Osmophobia**
Bogeymen: **Bogyphobia**
Books: **Bibliophobia**
Bridges: **Gephyrophobia**
Britishness: **Anglophobia**
Bullets: **Ballistophobia**
Bulls: **Taurophobia**
Burglars: **Scelerophobia**
Cats: **Galeophobia**
Cemeteries: **Coimetrophobia**
Chickens: **Alektorophobia**
Chins: **Geniophobia**
Chopsticks: **Consecotaleophobia**
Clocks/time: **Chronophobia**
Clothing: **Vestiphobia**
Clouds: **Nephophobia**
Clowns: **Coulrophobia**
Cold things: **Frigophobia**
Colors: **Chromophobia**
Comets: **Cometophobia**
Computers: **Cyberphobia**
Cooking: **Mageirocophobia**
Corpses: **Necrophobia**
Crossing streets: **Dromophobia**
Dancing: **Chorophobia**
Daylight/sunshine: **Phengophobia**
Decision-making: **Decidophobia**
Defeat: **Kakorrhaphiophobia**
Dentists: **Dentophobia**
Doctors: **Iatrophobia**
Dogs: **Cynophobia**
Dolls: **Pediophobia**
Dreams: **Oneirophobia**
Drinking: **Dipsophobia**
Dryness: **Xerophobia**
Dust: **Amathophobia**
Eating: **Phagophobia**
Eight (the number): **Octophobia**
Electricity: **Electrophobia**

TOUGH LUCK

AN EXPERIMENT IN FEAR

The instructions were simple: Spend twenty-four hours disobeying as many superstitions as possible, and do so on the thirteenth day of the month. A day that happened to be a Friday.

Who would ever volunteer for such an experiment? What bold soul would dare laugh in the face of Lady Luck? "Not me!" said Joshua Gee. "Give me ghosts any day. I can run away from them—and I frequently do! But bad luck will haunt me no matter where my duty takes me."

Fortunately for ENCYCLOPEDIA HORRIFICA, Investigator Gee finally obliged when his superiors informed him that the next five pages would be mostly blank if he didn't.

13
Friday
00:00 MIDNIGHT.
FRIDAY THE 13TH.

THE EXPERIMENT MUST BEGIN AT MY PRIVATE RESIDENCE. WILL NO PLACE BE SAFE? I REVIEW THE SUPERSTITIOUS TO-DO LIST PREPARED BY MY LOYAL HENCHMAN, THE MYSTERIOUS MISTER GRUTTY. FIRST ITEM: BEFORE RETIRING FOR THE NIGHT, CHANGE YOUR BEDSHEETS.

THIS WILL BRING BAD DREAMS. DONE . . . BUT I'LL GO TO BED LATER. MUCH LATER.

11:20 WOKE UP ONLY A FEW MINUTES AGO. DREAMED I WAS BEING ATTACKED BY CATS, THEN SLEPT THROUGH THREE ALARM CLOCKS. LEFT MY HAT ON THE BED ALL NIGHT AND PUT IT BACK ON WHILE STILL IN BED. BOTH ARE BIG NO-NO'S. PURPOSELY GOT OUT OF BED ON "THE WRONG SIDE" (THAT IS, THE SIDE OPPOSITE THE NORM). THE TEAM EXPECTED ME HOURS AGO AT HEADQUARTERS. THEY'LL ASSUME THE WORST.

12:10 STILL HAVEN'T MADE IT OUTSIDE, BUT DARED TO SHAVE ON THIS SURE-TO-BE-UNLUCKY DAY. NO PERMANENT SCARS.

12:30 PUT ON T-SHIRT INSIDE OUT, AS THE TO-DO LIST INSISTS. PULLED OFF THE TAG FROM A CRISP NEW REGULATION-BLACK INVESTIGATOR SHIRT AND PURPOSELY BUTTONED EACH BUTTON IN THE WRONG BUTTONHOLE. THE RIGHT SIDE OF THE SHIRT IS NOW LONGER THAN THE LEFT. IT LOOKS RATHER DASHING. IT WOULD APPEAR THAT A LOPSIDED SHIRT COMPLEMENTS MY CROOKED BODY QUITE NICELY. A NEW LOOK FOR ME?

13:00 THE THIRTEENTH HOUR OF FRIDAY THE 13TH! FEELING UNCERTAIN ABOUT LEAVING THE HOUSE. WHY GET INTO A THUMB WAR WITH THE FICKLE FINGER OF OLD MAN FATE?

13:30 STILL HAVEN'T OPENED THE DOOR. THE TIME IS NOW. BEFORE LEAVING, I DOUBLE-DARE FATE BY DROPPING MY KEYS AND MY UMBRELLA ON THE FLOOR, AS COMMANDED BY THE TO-DO LIST. PLUS, ONE MORE ITEM: OPEN THE UMBRELLA INDOORS. . . .

NOT I! NO WAY! NEVER!

OKAY, MAYBE FOR TEN SECONDS. JUST THIS ONCE. I SHUT MY EYES, TURN MY HEAD, AND HOLD IT FAR AWAY. FEELS LIKE HOLDING A TIME BOMB. TEN SECONDS PASS. I WAIT FOR SOMETHING BAD TO HAPPEN. THE BUILDING IS SILENT. NOTHING HAPPENS. SO FAR.

14:15 HALFWAY TO HQ, I SPOT SEVERAL WORKERS UNLOADING FURNITURE FROM A TRUCK. THEIR LADDER LEANS AGAINST SOME SCAFFOLDING. ON MY FIRST PASS, I DON'T QUITE MAKE IT UNDER THE LADDER. DRAT!

A standard-issue Paranormal Investigator Hat.

FEAR OF . . .

Everything: **Panophobia**
Eyes: **Ommatophobia**
Fainting: **Asthenophobia**
Feathers: **Pteronophobia**
Fire: **Pyrophobia**
Fish: **Ichthyophobia**
Floods: **Antlophobia**
Flowers: **Anthophobia**
Flutes: **Aulophobia**
Flying: **Aviophobia**
Foreign languages: **Xenoglossophobia**
Foreigners: **Xenophobia**
Forests: **Hylophobia**
Forests at night: **Nyctohylophobia**
Four (the number): **Tetraphobia**
Freezing to death: **Cryophobia**
Friday the 13th: **Paraskavedekatriaphobia**
Frogs: **Batrachophobia**
Garlic: **Alliumphobia**
Ghosts: **Phasmophobia**
Gold: **Aurophobia**
Good news: **Euphobia**
Gravity: **Barophobia**
Hair: **Trichophobia**
Halloween: **Samhainophobia**
Hands: **Chirophobia**
Handwriting: **Graphophobia**
Heat: **Thermophobia**
Heights: **Acrophobia**
Home: **Ecophobia**
Horses: **Equinophobia**
Hospitals: **Nosocomephobia**
Hurricanes/tornadoes: **Lilapsophobia**
Ideas: **Ideophobia**
Injections: **Trypanophobia**
Injury: **Traumatophobia**
Insects: **Entomophobia**
Itching: **Acarophobia**
Jumping: **Catapedaphobia**
Justice: **Dikephobia**
Knees: **Genuphobia**
Knowledge: **Epistemophobia**
Lakes: **Limnophobia**
Large things: **Megalophobia**
Laughter: **Geliophobia**
Learning: **Sophophobia**
Lice: **Pediculophobia**
Light: **Photophobia**
Looking up: **Anablephobia**
Loud noises: **Ligyrophobia**
Love: **Philophobia**
Machines: **Mechanophobia**
Meat: **Carnophobia**
Medications: **Pharmacophobia**
Memories: **Mnemophobia**
Men: **Androphobia**
Metal: **Metallophobia**
Meteors: **Meteorophobia**
Mice: **Musophobia**

WHY WON'T THESE LAZY, CHATTY WORKERS GET OUT OF MY WAY? I DOUBLE BACK. NEARLY TRIPPING TWO PEOPLE, I RUSH UNDER THE LADDER AND SCURRY AWAY WITHOUT MAKING EYE CONTACT. EASY!

14:20   STEPPED ON SEVENTY-SEVEN CRACKS SO FAR.

14:25   GRABBED BREAKFAST AT A CAFÉ. BEFORE SITTING DOWN TO EAT, I KNOCKED DOWN A CHAIR, LIFTED IT, PASSED IT OVER THE TABLE, AND ROTATED IT IN A COMPLETE CIRCLE, PER INSTRUCTIONS. ONLOOKERS APPEAR WORRIED. THE BLUEBERRY MUFFINS HERE ARE DELICIOUS.

14:50   PURCHASED A FULL-LENGTH MIRROR AND A TWO-POUND RUBBER MALLET.

15:00   FINALLY ARRIVE AT HQ AND IN ONE PIECE! NUMBER OF TRAMPLED CRACKS SO FAR: 107. I'VE ALSO ENTERED ELEVEN DOORWAYS LEFT-FOOT-FIRST.

15:15   THE BOSS OF OFFICIAL OPERATIONS INFORMS ME THAT WEARING GREEN BRINGS GRIEF. SHE LENDS ME HER GREEN SWEATER FOR ONE HOUR. I RESEARCH THE ASTONISHING BROWN LADY OF RAYNHAM HALL (SEE PAGE 58) AS I WAIT FOR THE BAD LUCK TO KICK IN.

15:45   RECEIVED A SPECIAL ASSIGNMENT WITH A $1000 PAYCHECK ATTACHED. IF THAT'S BAD LUCK, THEN I MUST REMEMBER TO INVEST IN AN ENTIRE RACK FULL OF GREEN SWEATERS TWO SIZES TOO SMALL. I RETURN THE NOW-SWEATY SWEATER TO THE BOSS. (IT WAS HOT IN THAT THING!) I TUCK A SALT SHAKER INTO MY JACKET FOR LATER.

16:45   THE MYSTERIOUS MISTER GRUTTY AND I ASCEND TO THE ROOF. OTHER WORKERS PASS US ON THE STAIRS. THE MYSTERIOUS MISTER GRUTTY WONDERS WHAT THEY MUST THINK OF TWO DETERMINED-LOOKING GENTLEMEN CARRYING A MALLET AND A MIRROR.
"JUST ACT NATURAL," I SAY. "THEY DON'T HAVE ANY REASON TO SUSPECT A THING."
BUT SECRETLY, I WONDER HOW THE OUTCOME OF TODAY'S EXPERIMENT WILL AFFECT THE LIVES OF THESE INNOCENT BYSTANDERS—NOT TO MENTION THE MYSTERIOUS MISTER GRUTTY. WILL MY BAD MOJO TOPPLE THE ENTIRE BUILDING?
MEMO TO HQ: THE MYSTERIOUS MISTER GRUTTY DESERVES A PAY RAISE.

16:56   A HIDEOUSLY SUNNY DAY OUTSIDE. WANT TO DETERMINE THE SAFEST PLACE TO POSITION THE MIRROR. SUDDENLY . . . CRAAASH! IT SLIPS FROM MY FINGERS!
"THAT'S SOME BAD LUCK," WHISPERS THE MYSTERIOUS MISTER GRUTTY, STARING DOWN AT A HUNDRED DANGEROUS SHARDS.
"WHAT'S THAT?"
"IT WAS A TRUE ACCIDENT. NOW YOU'RE REALLY IN TROUBLE. SEVEN YEARS, THEY SAY. . . ."
I'LL LET HIM CLEAN UP.

17:56 THE SUN SETTING ON FRIDAY THE 13TH, WE'VE LEFT HQ TO VISIT A LARGE PET EMPORIUM. THE SHOP OFFERS CAGED CATS IN GRAY, WHITE, AND MANY OTHER COLORS. TWO BLACK ONES RESIDE AT THE FAR END. ONE HAS WHITE PAWS, THOUGH. IF WE CROSS PATHS WITH THAT ONE, HAVE WE STILL PERFORMED OUR DUTY?

EAGER FOR OUR ATTENTION, THE OTHER, ALL-BLACK ONE POKES ITS PAW THROUGH THE BARS.

THE MYSTERIOUS MISTER GRUTTY MOTIONS TOWARD A STOUT OLD WOMAN WEARING AN EMPLOYEE BADGE. HER HAIR IS FRIZZY, AND SHE HAS MEAN EYES. "A PROFESSIONAL 'CAT LADY'!" HE POINTS OUT.

"CAN WE TAKE OUT A CAT AND HOLD IT?" I INNOCENTLY ASK HER.

"I DON'T KNOW," THE CAT LADY SAYS. "THE CAT MIGHT GET AWAY. IT HAPPENED ONCE BEFORE AND TOOK US FOREVER TO FIND IT IN THE STORE."

THE MYSTERIOUS MISTER GRUTTY AND I BOTH CHUCKLE AT THE THOUGHT OF THE LITTLE CRITTER RACING TOWARD FREEDOM. IT WOULD BE LIKE THE TV SHOW *PRISON BREAK!*

"IT WOULDN'T BE VERY FUNNY AT ALL," THE CAT LADY SAYS WITH A STERN FACE.

WE ARE DENIED ACCESS TO THE BLACK CAT'S PATH.

FEAR OF ...

Mirrors/reflections: **Eisoptrophobia**
Money: **Chrematophobia**
Moon: **Selenophobia**
Moths: **Mottephobia**
Motion: **Kinetophobia**
Mushrooms: **Mycophobia**
Music: **Melophobia**
Nakedness: **Gymnophobia**
Names: **Nomatophobia**
New things: **Neophobia**
Nighttime: **Nyctophobia**
Noise: **Acousticophobia**
Nosebleeds: **Epistaxiophobia**
Numbers: **Numerophobia**
Oceans: **Thalassophobia**
Odors: **Olfactophobia**
Old people: **Gerontophobia**
Open high places: **Aeroacrophobia**
Opinions: **Allodoxaphobia**
Otters: **Lutraphobia**
Pain: **Algophobia**
Paper: **Papyrophobia**
Parasites: **Parasitophobia**
Peanut butter sticking to the roof of the mouth: **Arachibutyrophobia**
Pee: **Urophobia**
People: **Anthropophobia**
Phobias: **Phobophobia**
Places, certain: **Topophobia**
Plants: **Botanophobia**
Pleasure: **Hedonophobia**
Poetry: **Metrophobia**
Poison: **Iophobia**
Politicians: **Politicophobia**
Poop: **Coprophobia**
Punishment: **Poinephobia**
Puppets: **Pupaphobia**
Purple (the color): **Porphyrophobia**
Rain: **Ombrophobia**
Red (the color): **Ereuthophobia**
Relatives: **Syngenesophobia**
Reptiles: **Herpetophobia**
Riding in cars: **Ochophobia**
Riding in vehicles: **Amaxophobia**
Rivers/running water: **Potamophobia**
School: **Scolionophobia**
Shadows: **Sciophobia**
Sharks: **Selachophobia**
Sharp objects: **Aichmophobia**
Shellfish: **Ostraconophobia**
Sitting down: **Kathisophobia**
Sleep: **Somniphobia**
Slime/mucus: **Blennophobia**
Small objects: **Tapinophobia**
Snakes: **O...**

WHAT NEXT? OUTSIDE, I SPOT A SUBWAY STATION AND MENTION THE WORDS "BLACK RAT." ALAS, EVEN THE MYSTERIOUS MISTER GRUTTY WILL GO ONLY SO FAR IN THE NAME OF SCIENCE. HIS PARTING WORDS: "SEE YOU ON MONDAY . . . I HOPE!"

18:37 TOTAL NUMBER OF CRACKS TRAMPLED TODAY: 199.

19:30 BACK AT HQ, I FINISH CLIPPING MY FINGERNAILS. IT'S BAD LUCK TO DO THIS ON FRIDAYS. AM PLEASED TO DISCOVER NO LIFE-THREATENING HANGNAILS.

20:20 DINNER TIME. ARRIVE AT A RESTAURANT CALLED RICE WITH AN ASSOCIATE NAMED JOSH. A LONG LINE AT THE DOOR, BUT WE ARE INSTANTLY SEATED AT ONE EMPTY TABLE JUST BIG ENOUGH FOR TWO JOSHES. IS MY LUCK IMPROVING?

20:35 TAKING THE SALT SHAKER FROM MY JACKET, I NOTIFY JOSH THAT I MUST SPILL SALT ON THE TABLE BEFORE EATING. I BREAK THE NEWS ABOUT TODAY'S EXPERIMENT—AND HOW IT MIGHT AFFECT JOSH'S OWN FATE. HE HANDLES IT WELL. SOON AFTER, I KNOCK ON WOOD FOR GOOD LUCK, PURELY OUT OF HABIT.

"NAH-UH," JOSH SAYS. "YOU'RE NOT ALLOWED TO DO THAT TODAY."

"OH, THAT'S RIGHT," I SAY, THE STRESS OF THE EXPERIMENT CLEARLY TAKING ITS TOLL ON MY MEMORY.

I MENTION HOW MANY TIMES I NEARLY GOT RUN OVER BY TRAFFIC TODAY WHILE STARING AT THE PAVEMENT IN SEARCH OF CRACKS TO TRAMPLE. ALWAYS A MAN OF REASON, JOSH POINTS OUT THAT MANY SUPERSTITIONS CAN PROBABLY BE TRACED BACK TO PERFECTLY REASONABLE FEARS. ALTHOUGH CRACKED SIDEWALKS POSE LITTLE HARM IN THIS NEIGHBORHOOD, STEPPING ON UNSTABLE GROUND CAN BE QUITE DANGEROUS IN OTHER SITUATIONS. ANOTHER EXAMPLE: LADDERS CAN BE WOBBLY, SO WALKING UNDERNEATH ONE ALWAYS POSES A RISK. ESPECIALLY FOR THE PERSON CLIMBING IT? ENERGIZED BY THIS SUDDEN INJECTION OF COMMON SENSE, I POUR THE SALT ON THE TABLE. STRANGELY, NOTHING COMES OUT. EVEN AFTER I TAP IT HARD AGAINST THE WALL.

"EXCUSE ME," I SAY. OUTSIDE THE RESTAURANT, I SMASH THE SALT SHAKER INTO THE SIDEWALK. THE SHAKER SPLITS IN HALF TO REVEAL THE SALT WAS COMPLETELY SOLID. THE ONLY WORD FOR A CURSED CONDIMENT LIKE THAT IS "UNLUCKY."

20:40 FUNNY ENOUGH, MY MEAL COULD USE SOME SALT, BUT I DON'T SAY ANYTHING.

21:06 NEXT ON THE TO-DO LIST: A SLOW CRUNCHING NOISE—LIKE THE BREAKING OF A RODENT'S SPINE— AS I SNAP APART A CHOPSTICK AND INSERT IT UPRIGHT INTO MY FOOD.

21:28 "WHAT IS THIS?" ASKS THE FURIOUS WAITRESS WIPING AWAY TINY WHITE ROCKS AND BROKEN BITS OF PLASTIC.

"I THINK IT'S . . . SALT?" I SAY, SQUINTING CLOSELY.

"SALT? DID YOU DO THIS?"

"NO."

"THIS ISN'T YOUR SALT?" SHE ASKS, LIKE A TEACHER INTERROGATING THE KID WHO BRINGS HIS NUNCHUCKS TO SCHOOL.

"NO, I FOUND IT ON THE FLOOR."

FINALLY, HER ENTIRE FACE RELAXES.

"WHY WOULD I BRING MY OWN SALT?" I ASK WITH A LAUGH. "YOU THINK I TRAVEL WITH MY OWN SALT?"

SHE GIGGLES. "NO, YOU'RE RIGHT? WEIRD—I DON'T KNOW WHERE IT CAME FROM. . . ."

AFTER SHE LEAVES, I CHECK OFF THE FINAL ITEM ON THE LIST: LIE THROUGH YOUR TEETH WITHOUT CROSSING YOUR FINGERS.

13 Fri

14 Saturday

MISSION ACCOMPLISHED!

MIDNIGHT HOME AGAIN! NOT A SCRATCH ON ME, AND CLEAN BEDSHEETS, TOO. SEVEN YEARS BEGIN RIGHT NOW.

Investigator Gee reported that he was sneezing and sniffling for the rest of the night. Was it bad luck? Probably not. He is extremely allergic to cats—no matter what color they are.

FEAR OF . . .

Spaces, confined: **Claustrophobia**
Spaces, empty: **Kenophobia**
Spaces, open: **Agoraphobia**
Speaking: **Lalophobia**
Speaking in public: **Glossophobia**
Speed: **Tachophobia**
Spiders: **Arachnophobia**
Stairs: **Climacophobia**
Standing up: **Stasiphobia**
Stars: **Astrophobia**
Stings: **Cnidophobia**
Stories/lies: **Mythophobia**
String: **Linonophobia**
Surgery: **Tomophobia**
Symbols: **Symbolophobia**
Symmetry: **Symmetrophobia**
Tapeworms: **Teniophobia**
Technology: **Technophobia**
Teenagers: **Ephebiphobia**
Teeth: **Odontophobia**
Telephones: **Telephonophobia**
Termites: **Isopterophobia**
Test-taking: **Testophobia**
Theaters: **Theatrophobia**
Thinking: **Phronemophobia**
Thirteen (the number): **Triskadekaphobia**
Thunder storms: **Brontophobia**
Tiredness: **Kopophobia**
Tombstones: **Placophobia**
Tornadoes/hurricanes: **Lilapsophobia**
Touching: **Aphenphosmphobia**
Trains: **Siderodromophobia**
Travel: **Hodophobia**
Trees: **Dendrophobia**
Trembling: **Ttremophobia**
Tyrants: **Tyrannophobia**
Ugliness: **Cacophobia**
Vegetables: **Lachanophobia**
Ventriloquist's dummies **Automatonophobia**
Voices: **Phonophobia**
Vomiting: **Emetophobia**
Waiting for a long time: **Macrophobia**
Walking: **Ambulophobia**
Washing: **Ablutophobia**
Wasps: **Spheksophobia**
Water: **Aquaphobia**
Weakness: **Asthenophobia**
Wealth: **Plutophobia**
White (the color): **Leukophobia**
Wind: **Anemophobia**
Women: **Gynophobia**
Words: **Logophobia**
Work: **Ergophobia**
Worms: **Scoleciphobia**
Writing in public: **Scriptophobia**
X-rays: **Radiophobia**
Yellow (the color): **Xanthophobia**

THE FORBIDDEN bookshelf!

YOU WON'T BELIEVE YOUR EYES ... OR OURS.

MOST HORRIFIC PRE-*FRANKENSTEIN* FRANKENSTEIN

In *The Sand-Man* (1816), E. T. A. Hoffman wrote of a human-size doll named Olimpia, who is brought to life by a mad scientist named Coppelius. Olimpia loses her eyes during a quarrel between several actual humans. In 1818, Mary Shelley published *Frankenstein*, also about a scientist, a nonhuman, and body parts aplenty.

MOST HORRIFIC PRE-*DRACULA* DRACULA

Nearly eighty years before the novel *Dracula*, Dr. John William Polidori thrilled readers with *The Vampyre*, about a nobleman who sinks his teeth into London's nightlife.

MOST HORRIFIC WRITERS OF THE 20TH CENTURY

WRITER	WICKED PICK
Ray Bradbury	*Something Wicked This Way Comes*
Shirley Jackson	"The House on Haunted Hill"
Stephen King	*Cycle of the Werewolf*
H. P. Lovecraft	"The Dunwich Horror"

MOST HORRIFIC WRITER OF ANY CENTURY

Other horror writers fear Edgar Allan Poe (1809—1849), your grandparents' grandparents feared Edgar Allan Poe, and you should fear him, too. Why? "The Raven," "The Pit and the Pendulum," "The Tell-Tale Heart," and many other reasons.

MYSTERIES OF THE UNKNOWN
The UFO Phenomenon
TIME-LIFE BOOKS

MYSTERIES OF THE UNKNOWN
Mysterious Creatures
TIME-LIFE BOOKS

THE WORLD OF THE UNEXPLAINED   JANET AND COLIN BORD
TIME-LIFE BOOKS

16561-9

TIME-LIFE BOOKS

GRAMERCY

SCHMITT

UNITED STATES AIR FORCE
SEARCH AND RESCUE
SURVIVAL TRAINING   AF REGULATION 64-4
REPRINT OF DEPARTMENT OF THE AIR FORCE FIELD MANUAL
BARNES & NOBLE BOOKS

Carter and Mace   THE DISCOVERY OF THE TOMB OF TUTANKHAMEN   Dover 0-486-23500-9

FAIRY & FOLK TALES of IRELAND   W. B. YEATS

MAX BROOKS   THE ZOMBIE SURVIVAL GUIDE

Stories in STONE   A Field Guide to Cemetery Symbolism and Iconography   KEISTER   mjf

In Search of

LOREN COLEMAN & JEROME CLARK   Cryptozoology A to Z

NICKELL   REAL-LIFE X-Files   KENTUCKY

Fort   The Complete Books of Charles Fort   Dover 0-486-23094-5

CASSELL's dictionary of superstitions   david pickering   CASSELL

TOR   READING THE ENEMY'S MIND   INSIDE STAR GATE: AMERICA'S PSYCHIC ESPIONAGE PROGRAM   PAUL H. SMITH   0-817-57853-4 $7.99 ($10.99 CAN)

A Paranormal Casebook   Auerbach   Atriad Press

GULEY   THE ENCYCLOPEDIA OF GHOSTS and SPIRITS   SECOND EDITION   Checkmark Books

STEIGER   REAL GHOSTS, RESTLESS SPIRITS, AND HAUNTED PLACES   VISIBLE INK

BARING-GOULD   THE BOOK OF WEREWOLVES   DOVER

KAL K. KORFF

THE BEAST OF GEVAUDAN   ABBÉ PIERRE POURCHER   TRANSLATED BY DEREK BROCKIS

WELL UFO CRASH

NASA SP-419   The Search for Extraterrestrial Intelligence   SETI

Bondeson   The FEEJEE MERMAID   and Other Essays in Natural and Unnatural History

IN SEARCH of DRACULA   Raymond T. McNally & Radu Florescu   Houghton Mifflin

EH

SPECIAL INVESTIGATION

NEW YORK CITY—Jonathan Valuckas does not know how to communicate with an ancient, undead "squid-dragon," but he acts like he does.

In a play entitled *Metronoma*, Mr. Valuckas (pictured below) has spent night after night grappling with monsters and madness. The role requires a familiarity with forbidden books; a suit and tie like those worn in the 1930s; and a fondness for one of the most influential horror writers of all time: H. P. Lovecraft (1890—1937).

"He has so many devoted fans for the same reason that Harry Potter and Star Wars are popular," explains Mr. Valuckas after a performance. "He created a fully defined world with a set of rules,

SUBJECT: Monstrously popular author H. P. Lovecraft

MISSION: To find out if an evil book described by Lovecraft was actually real

IN SEARCH OF: *The Necronomicon*

LOCATION: The Ontological Theater

MEMO TO HEADQUARTERS: This book report is unlike any you've read before—unless your name is "Cthulhu of the Old Ones."

and it was believable. It was the first time anybody did that in horror."

The rules of Lovecraft's world even come with an instruction book, and that book is what summons ENCYCLOPEDIA HORRIFICA to this cramped downtown theater at midnight. We seek a copy of what Lovecraft called *The Necronomicon*. The title means "The

Ph'nglui mglw'nafh Cthulhu

Book of the Dead," and it's one book you can definitely judge by its cover. In stories such as "The Dunwich Horror" and "The Call of Cthulhu"—as well as a scholarly essay entitled "History of *The Necronomicon*"—Lovecraft writes of doomed men ill-advisedly reciting its secret passages and reviving long-dead creatures eager to rule the Earth....

So naturally we hoped to pick up a copy!

Alas, the terrible text featured in *Metronoma* is just an old coffee-table book. Mr. Valuckas is certain *The Necronomicon* isn't available at the local library, either.

Did *The Necronomicon* exist during Lovecraft's time? No, says the man who plays him.

Not even in paperback?

"He made it up," says Mr. Valuckas. "And he did a really good job." 🕷

Never content to let sleeping monsters lie, we put down our horror books (only briefly!) and picked up our history books. Might we find "Books of the Dead" in distant times and places? The answer is yes!

In ancient Egypt, the dead were frequently laid to rest alongside papyri (paper-like pages) and symbolic artwork intended to guide them on their journey in the afterlife. A common name for these collected texts translated to "The Book of Going Forth by Day," but over time, Egyptologists began saying "The Book of the Dead," which is far catchier, don't you think?

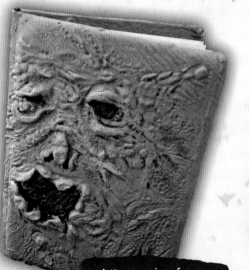

A Necronomicon from a Hollywood movie.

In this "Book of the Dead," two souls (far left) will be punished for any misdeeds by a foul hippo-croco-lion.

R'lyeh wgah'nagl fhtagn. 🕷

🕷 In monster-speak, this means, "In his house at R'lyeh, dead Cthulhu waits dreaming."

FATE

SPRING
1948
25¢

VOLUME 1   NUMBER 1

THE TRUTH ABOUT
THE FLYING SAUCERS
By KENNETH ARNOLD

MARK TWAIN AND
HALLEY'S COMET
By HAROLD M. SHERMAN

INVISIBLE BEINGS
WALK THE EARTH
By R. J. CRESCENZI

TWENTY MILLION
MANIACS
By G. H. IRWIN

Many Other Startling
Articles And Features

The FLYING DISKS

Some people collect Transformers. Others keep toenail clippings. We here at horrific headquarters prefer to collect things that are older and crumblier—such as back issues of *Fate* magazine.

Never heard of it? Well, you might recognize the name Kenneth Arnold. He was mentioned on page 21 of the very book you hold now. Thanks to Issue #1 of *Fate* magazine (shown here, actual size), the whole world learned all about Mr. Arnold's amazing story, and the editors of *Fate* (including Loyd "Professor Paranormal" Auerbach) have chronicled countless more amazing stories for six decades now.

Part Four

Fate is more than a magazine. It's also a word meaning "something awful that will happen in the future."

Judging solely on the basis of the next chapters, our forecasts predict the future will be cloudy with a 100% chance of awful. Within mere moments, expect to be zombified, tricked, cursed, and possibly buried. And that's on page 108 alone!

You're nearing the end, friends.
Here await four...

Fearsome Fates

TO BE OR NOT ZOMBIE!

THERE'S JUST SOMETHING ABOUT ZOMBIES....

8 THINGS YOU NEED TO KNOW ABOUT ZOMBIES

#8 In 1968, filmmaker George A. Romero debuted *Night of the Living Dead*. It inspired countless horror movies to come, and it still scares the heebie-jeebies out of the living today.

#7 Hollywood zombies are often portrayed as being extremely slow. They pose a threat only because they don't know when to give up, and there are usually too many of them to ignore.

#6 Not all zombie movies have scary titles. For example, *The Incredibly Strange Creatures Who Stopped Living and Became Mixed-Up Zombies* (1964).

#5

Zombies Ate My Neighbors was one of the first video games to star the walking dead. The goal of this 1993 Konami game is to defeat a final boss named Dr. Tongue, who spews deadly tongues at any attackers.

#4

Thanks to the *Resident Evil* series, zombies helped popularize a type of video game called "survival horror," in which gamers usually find themselves tiptoeing into dark places with as much ammo as possible.

#3

In *The Zombie Survival Guide* and *World War Z*, two hugely popular books by Max Brooks, a contagious disease turns people into zombies. In other zombie stories, causes range from toxic chemicals to radiation to alien mind control.

#2

"Zombie walks" (pictured above) are an increasingly popular way to liven up any parade. Or shall we say "deaden" up? Either way, give the girls a hand!

1962: A man by the name of Clairvius Narcisse is declared dead by the Albert Schweitzer Hospital on the island of Haiti. His family attends his funeral and says good-bye.

1980: On a sunny spring day, a desperate individual appears in the late Mr. Narcisse's hometown. He looks like Mr. Narcisse. He acts like Mr. Narcisse. And strangest of all, he claims to be Mr. Narcisse!

#1

ZOMBIES ARE REAL!

Well, not the Hollywood kind. But "*zombis*" are a different matter....

Was this man the walking dead? In a sense, he might have been. There was certainly no reason to believe he was an impostor. At least one doctor reportedly identified the man as Clairvius Narcisse, and so did Mr. Narcisse's family.

When asked where he had been for so long, Mr. Narcisse claimed that his own brother had turned him into a *zombi*, a fearsome fate described in Haitian folklore for centuries. In this instance, Mr. Narcisse believed he had been mistaken for dead because a group of wicked men (led by his brother!) had severely drugged him. He was later awakened by the same men, fed more poisons, and put to work without getting paid.

After finally escaping in 1964, Mr. Narcisse spent sixteen years hiding out from his brother. As you might have guessed by now, the two of them didn't get along very well, so only when the brother passed away did Mr. Narcisse finally reappear.

In 1983, Mr. Narcisse was interviewed by *Time* magazine. During his time as a *zombi* worker, "the slightest chore required great effort," he said. The poisons made him feel as though his "eyes were turned in."

Z-Speak

Although the two official languages in Haiti are Creole and French, you don't have to learn either one to speak *zombi*. Some useful terms:

A *zombi z'outil* is the name for a victim confined to an urban workshop.

A *zombi jardin* tends to his master's garden, which might be an okay summer job if it weren't for the part about feeling half dead.

To cure a *zombi*, you'll need to turn him or her into a *zombi gâté* ("spoiled zombi"). How? Haitian folklore recommends feeding salt to the victim, but scientists disagree. There is no reason to believe that salt works as an antidote for the alleged *zombi* poisons. Our best advice: Avoid becoming a *zombi* to begin with.

In 1835, Haiti passed an anti-zombification law. According to Article 246 of the Haitian Penal Code, giving somebody a poison that causes extreme sleepiness is regarded as attempted murder. If the victim is buried in that state, it's an act of murder.

TOXIC

You might be wondering why there's a picture of a plant in a chapter called "To Be or Not Zombie!" Turn the page to find out.

Solaneae.

Datura Stramonium L.

W.Müller a.d. Nat.

A Recipe for Doom

Ethnobotanist Wade Davis is anything but a zombie. He has a passion for plants, world cultures, and the pursuit of adventure. For those three reasons, he packed his bags in 1982 and traveled to Haiti in response to alleged "*zombi* poisons."

"We didn't know what—if anything—was in this preparation that had been long rumored to exist," he told ENCYCLOPEDIA HORRIFICA. "Initially, I assumed it might be a toxic plant, but we weren't just looking for a poisonous plant. There are lots of poisonous plants. However, there are not very many toxins that can bring on a state of apparent death so profound that it can fool a physician."

So what exactly is the recipe for a *zombi* poison? Mr. Davis, author of 1985's *The Serpent and the Rainbow*, reveals that the datura plant (pictured on page 109) was contained in some of the *zombi* poison samples he analyzed. When eaten, this toxic plant can cause confusion and memory loss.

Before listing more toxins, Mr. Davis explains that he thinks one of the most important secret ingredients is not what people ate or applied to their skin. It's what they believed. That is to say, if your mind believes very strongly in zombiism, then your body is more likely to become zombified by the poisons.

"I saw the degree to which, in the Haitian rural society, these beliefs manifested as physical properties, or attributes, before my eyes. And I don't care what *anybody* says about the Leidenfrost effect,＊ I certainly can't put a hot burning coal in my mouth without it ruining my mouth. Yet I saw people doing it all the time."

＊ The theory that a layer of steam can protect whatever comes in contact with something very, very hot.

TOXIC

Pieces of the deadly cane toad (*Bufo marinus*) are thought to be contained in some *zombi* poisons.

Another ingredient contained in some *zombi* poisons was a dangerous chemical called tetrodotoxin. Found inside the organs of the puffer fish, it can paralyze the human body—or kill it. Mr. Davis says it all depends on how much poison has entered the victim's body.

Believe it or not, the puffer fish is listed on many restaurant menus in Japan. It's called fugu sashimi.

"Fugu has been eaten for generations in Japan," says Mr. Davis. "Because of that, it's quite understood exactly what the toxin does. In fact, in Japan, there are cases of people nailed into coffins by mistake and other cases of people being laid out by the grave for three days to make sure they were really dead."

TOXIC

Tricked by Pixies!

FAERIE TALES CAN BE SCARY TALES.

Question:
Which one of these is a faerie?

A.

B.

Answer:
Keep reading...

These days, humankind gets along pretty well with the faerie kind. We often think of faerie folk as little, happy-go-lucky things with wings, but this has not always been the case.

If you survived your encounter with the *bean-nighe*, or banshee, on page 6, then maybe you already want to panic at the sight of pixie dust. The creator of Count Dracula probably did! Imagine growing up in Ireland and hearing about a shriveled old hag who washes the clothes of those about to die. The moral of that story: Find your soapy socks by the stream and laundry day will be your last day.

In ancient Norse mythology, there were *ljósálfar* ("Light Elves") and *dökkálfar* ("Dark Elves"). Light Elves were the type of good-natured sprites you'd expect to meet on a ride at Walt Disney World. The Dark Elves would have torn Tinkerbell limb from limb. Perhaps they were cranky because they came from the humblest of origins. Storytellers say the Dark Elves evolved from the maggots crawling inside the giant Ymir's corpse.

That's why the answer to the pop quiz above is not A or B. It's "Both." You might call it a trick question, which leads us to a common trait among those who dwell in the realm of the fae: By all accounts, the faerie folk are notorious pranksters. They delight in making humans feel foolish.

Little do the little ones know: Even without their assistance, we humans are perfectly good at feeling foolish. Such is the fate of the paranormal investigator who does not beware of hoaxes—or anybody who forgets to check the calendar on April Fool's Day.

Fooled by Mother Nature

Whether pixie trick or optical illusion, this slouching tree trunk looks oddly human. Long ago, some faerie folk were said to manifest as trees and other plant life.

Similarly, certain mushrooms tend to grow in patterns shaped like circles or half-circles. These so-called "fairy rings" inspired folklore about forest faeries dancing in circles. Some fairy rings are believed to be over 600 years old.

A Famous Author Finds Faeries

Finding photographic evidence of faeries is no easy task. Take it from us. We left no toadstool unturned while researching this chapter. So imagine our shock when we learned that two ordinary schoolgirls had seemingly achieved the impossible.

In 1917, cousins Elsie Wright and Frances Griffiths were fond of playing outside in the village of Cottingley, England. One location in particular had everything Elsie and Frances could want in a meeting place, including sunlight, a tiny waterfall, and according to them, flying pixies and dancing gnomes! One day in July, the girls decided to bring back proof. Elsie showed her father a photograph that she said she had taken near the waterfall. It featured Frances and four tiny, jubilant winged figures that looked exactly like faerie folk.

It was to be the first of five similar photographs. The images might not still matter today if they had been deemed hoaxes, but surprisingly, they weren't! This is due largely to an author who was perhaps a little too eager to believe in unlikely phenomena: Sir Arthur Conan Doyle, the successful and well-regarded creator of Sherlock Holmes. In December 1920, *The Strand Magazine* published the girls' first two photos and an article by Doyle in which he declared the photos to be authentic. Although he cited the testimony of "two expert photographers" to back up his claims, even Doyle himself stated, "The cry of 'fake' is sure to be raised."

Of course, he was right about that last part—in time.

Amazingly, the two girls had outwitted the man who had invented the world's greatest detective, and for decades, many faerie fans continued to believe in the hoax. During their adult years, Elsie and Frances would seldom comment on the images. Even by the 1970s, they were hesitant to fess up. When a television crew asked, "Are they trick photographs?" Elsie's reply was: "I'd rather leave that open if you don't mind."

Ten-year-old Frances Griffiths took this photo of Elsie Wright during the summer of 1917. On the left is Elsie, who was sixteen at the time. On the right is a gnome—or so thought the author of the Sherlock Holmes mysteries.

Can YOU Find Faeries?

Most experts agree that Frances and Elsie used paper cutouts and double-exposure techniques to create their faerie "evidence." Reportedly, Frances always insisted that the fifth and final photograph (above) was the one image that was genuine.

The Top Five Most
HORRIFIC HOAXES

5. During medieval times, *The Travels of Sir John Mandeville*, a popular book, described places where one-eyed giants and dog-headed humans dwelled. Although it was mostly fiction, readers were led to believe it was mostly fact!

4. How do you preserve a baby dragon? Fill a thirty-inch jar with formaldehyde solution and begin hunting for the nearest dragon's nest. Only you'll be searching a long, long time because the pickled dragon (pictured here) was a rubber hoax. Photos of it were used to promote a fantasy novel in 2004.

3. On March 31, 1940, the Franklin Institute Science Museum announced that the world was going to end in twenty-four hours. Obviously, their numbers were waaaaay off, and they knew it, too. The employee responsible for the doomsday hoax was soon fired by the Philadelphia museum.

2. It's a good thing that the hotheaded naked ice borer was an April Fool's prank because you wouldn't want to meet one in real life. According to a fake April 1995 article in *Discover* magazine, "about a dozen small, hairless pink molelike creatures" were preying upon innocent penguins near the South Pole.

1. *The War of the Worlds*: A timeless science-fiction story about us versus the aliens. First, it was an 1898 book by H.G. Wells. Then, in 1938, it became a radio performance featuring false "news flashes" and lots of unearthly sound effects. And next—it became a street riot! Radio listeners were so fooled by the broadcast that 1.2 million of them fled the area of Grovers Mill, New Jersey, where the "invasion" was supposedly taking place. One man even fired a rifle at a water tower because he mistook it for a gigantic Martian robot!

Say Hello to Your Little Friends

Amidst all this flighty talk of faeries and hoaxes, ENCYCLOPEDIA HORRIFICA went on the hunt for teensy terrors that exist in real life. As it turns out, we didn't need to look any farther than our own eyelashes, and neither do you!

Inside your hair follicles are microscopic critters called mites. Close up, mites aren't very pretty, but most species don't harm the human body. Some of them are even helpful. Demodex mites, for example, eat the dead cells and other icky debris that accumulate on eyelashes and eyebrows. Sounds "mighty" tasty, no?

Magnified 240 times, this image is scientific proof of how ugly mites can be.

An eyelash mite in its natural habitat: your skin.

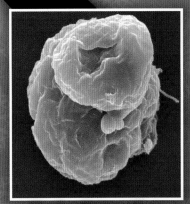
The digestive excretions of a dust mite, meaning "mite poop"!

117

THE CURSE OF THE MUMMY!

UNRAVEL THE MYSTERY OF A GRAVE MISFORTUNE.

"I TOLD YOU SO," read the front page of *The New York World* newspaper on March 24, 1923. Beneath that heading was a picture of Marie Corelli, a famous author who had many superstitious views on the subject of curses. In a brief article, Ms. Corelli described how a wealthy gentleman named Lord Carnarvon was seriously ill due to an infected mosquito bite, and by all accounts, this was true.

Also true: One year earlier, Lord Carnarvon and his partner, Howard Carter, had opened the tomb of King Tutankhamen, an ancient Egyptian pharaoh.

Big mistake—if you believe in curses, at least. And at the time, many did. People spoke of a bone-chilling threat scrawled upon Tut's sarcophagus: DEATH COMES ON WINGS TO HE WHO ENTERS THE TOMB OF A PHARAOH. So when Lord Carnarvon died soon after Ms. Corelli's article was published, who could blame some folks for getting all wrapped up in stories of a mummy's curse? Like all superstitious beliefs, curses provide easy answers to questions about tough topics like death and illness.

Does that mean all curses are real? Not necessarily . . .

Although ancient Egyptians did actually try to scare off grave robbers by decorating their tombs with fierce threats, none of the hieroglyphs in Tut's tomb translated to death-on-wings. And although Lord Carnarvon did die on April 5, 1923, he had been in poor health long before he entered Tut's tomb. And although Mr. Carter was the one responsible for first locating the site, the archaeologist lived a happy and healthy life until he died many years later at the age of sixty-four.

The mummy's curse: a lot of hot air. Other curses? Decide for yourself . . .

The body of King Tut, laid to rest in 1323 B.C.

DIGGING FOR TROUBLE

Gun-toting adventure-seekers like Lara Croft (pictured) and Indiana Jones lead some people to believe that archaeology is much more dangerous than it actually is. Real archaeologists are simply detectives who study ancient evidence to learn about human history. Even so, tombs are not the safest of workplaces.

- Dangerous natural gases like radon can build up inside enclosed spaces over time.
- Bad for the lungs, *Aspergillus flavus* is a species of toxic mold found inside some mummies.
- Archaeologists who dig in the soil all day are likely to encounter many types of poisonous fungi.
- *Pseudomonas* and *Staphylococcus* are infectious bacteria that might coat the walls of some tombs.

Because they believed all creatures still needed bodies in the afterlife, the ancient Egyptians also mummified the remains of baboons, cats, birds, and other animals.

According to The Artist's Handbook of Materials and Techniques, there was once a paint color called "Mummy" ... made from actual, ground-up mummies.

In 2006, police investigated a Michigan woman who tried to sell an unusual medical specimen on the auction Web site eBay: a 200-year-old mummy.

Fiery Temper

Steal rocks, shells, or sand from the Hawaiian Volcanoes National Park and you might end up wishing you'd bought a souvenir snow globe instead. According to local lore, the fire goddess Pele punishes anybody who takes anything from her sunny shores. Whether that's true or not, park rangers often receive packages containing debris from the beach and letters of apology written by down-on-their-luck tourists.

KILAUEA HAWAII

HAWAII

The Point Is to Do Harm

YULARA NT AUSTRALIA

Arriving in Australia? One thing you should never do is wave a bone or stick in the direction of a stranger. The Aboriginal people call this practice "pointing the bone." Combined with the right chant, it will put a curse on the person at whom you're pointing. The Aborigines also believe that you must follow the procedure very closely. Make a mistake, they say, and the victim will be you.

TURKEY

TÜRKIYE

Stare-Wear

In Turkey, this *nazar boncuğu*, or "evil eye amulet," will protect you against anybody whose mean gaze has the power to inflict harm.

QUICK! LOOK AWAY!*

In truth, it is unlikely that you face any danger by simply *looking* at the Hope Diamond. After all, millions of tourists view it every year at the National Museum of Natural History in Washington, DC, and nobody ever complains of feeling cursed when they leave. Alas, previous owners of this 45.52-carat diamond didn't fare as well, according to some reports. Museum officials regard the curse of the Hope Diamond as a myth. Even if you do, too, it's still a sight worth seeing: It's the largest gem of its kind in the world.

🕷 Just kidding.

Some people believe baseball diamonds can be cursed, too....

NO FAIR!

Fate doesn't always play by the rules.

NFL star Shaun Alexander injured a bone in his left foot soon after appearing on the cover of the *Madden NFL 07* video game. Mr. Alexander was supposedly the latest victim of the annual Madden Curse dating back to *Madden NFL 2000*.

The dreaded *Sports Illustrated* Cover Jinx has befallen numerous teams and players since Eddie Mathews broke his hand after appearing on the cover of Issue #1 in 1954.

Sports Illustrated

NFL Pl

An NHL
Battle w

The Cover that No One Would Pose for

Is the SI Jinx for Real?

JANUARY 21, 2002 www.cnnsi.com
AOL Keyword: Sports Illustrated

The Chicago Cubs haven't played in a World Series since 1945. Some fans blame it on a tavern owner named Billy Sianis. Mr. Sianis was tossed out of Wrigley Field for bringing his foul-smelling pet goat, so he reportedly initiated the Curse of the Billy Goat. Similarly, the Boston Red Sox suffered from the Curse of the Bambino for eight decades after they sold the legendary Babe Ruth (a.k.a. The Great Bambino).

SPECIAL INVESTIGATION

SUBJECT: Dudleytown

MISSION: To venture into a forest that is said to be cursed

IN SEARCH OF: Any evidence of a once-thriving colonial settlement

LOCATION: Somewhere in New England

MEMO TO HEADQUARTERS: Two centuries of tragedy. Curse or coincidence?

During most Special Investigations, ENCYCLOPEDIA HORRIFICA reports from a specific place, but in this instance, a specific place is what we're seeking. Historians call it Dudleytown. Superstitious types call it cursed.

Dudleytown was named after Abiel Dudley, Barzillai Dudley, and other early residents of the same last name. Their alleged troubles began in England. According to published reports, three Dudleys were beheaded by British kings and another accidentally infected thousands of his countrymen with the plague. Understandably eager for a fresh start, Dudleys began arriving in America in 1747. From then on, the tiny farming community of Dudleytown reaped little more than tales of murder, disease, and madness, if you believe storytellers of today. By 1900, the cold New England hilltop was largely deserted.

ENCYCLOPEDIA HORRIFICA won't comment on whether or not we located the site—with only a crude map and a short-tempered college student to guide the way. Nor will we describe how such an expedition might occur on a cloudy, eerily motionless Friday afternoon, when weather forecasters were predicting a heavy downpour at any moment. And we certainly won't invite you to join us as we stumble our way across the strange, slippery rock formation that some call Witches Dam.

After hiking up the barely there trail for ninety minutes, rainfall and nightfall would probably conspire to prevent you from finding the end of

spot the foundations of many long-abandoned stone cottages along the way.

Could this happen to my town someday? you might wonder, but only at first. Quickly, you'd notice how this rocky, shadowy territory was never ideal for farming—or anything else.

"Perhaps here, as in so many places, horror lies in the eye of the beholder," you might write in your research journal. Soon after, the rain would finally fall, and your only mission would be the journey back to a warm place called HQ. 💀

Dudleytown is currently

GRUESOME GOOD-BYES!

A BIOGRAPHY OF DEATH? NO, A DIE-OGRAPHY!

Meet Death. It's not evil. It's just doing its job.

The American Medical Association officially defines Death in two ways. It's what happens when a person's lungs stop functioning and the blood stops flowing, or it can occur when the entire brain deactivates.

Other, more symbolic visions of Death have existed since the dawn of civilization. Just like the Bogeymen on pages 90 and 91, Death is a fear that wears a thousand different faces. Death has been brought to life by poets and authors, artists and musicians, filmmakers and now even video game developers.

A few of those visions are presented here. Don't bother saying hello. Death only says good-bye.

A DAY IN THE LIFE OF DEATH

Population of Earth:
More than **6,500,000,000**
Average number of deaths per day:
152,029
Average number of deaths per hour:
6,335
Average number of deaths per minute:
106
Worldwide, an average of ten people died in the time it took you to read this sentence. The good news: Twice that many people were just born.

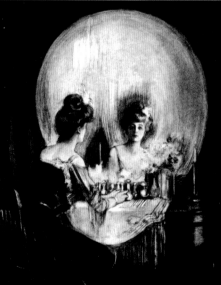

DEATH OR DECEPTION?
One of the oldest and most common symbols of Death is the human skull. Is Death hiding in this 1892 painting?

"HAPPY DEATHDAY!"
Figurines like the one pictured above are a common sight in Mexico, where Death comes once a year, every year, on the *Día de los Muertos* ("Day of the Dead"). During this festive occasion, skeleton figurines, or *calacas*, remind families that Death is a natural and vital part of human life.

AND INTRODUCING...

THE GRIM REAPER!

Today, Death often appears in movies and TV shows as the Grim Reaper, a skeletal figure in a black, hooded cloak. Clearly, he's not very fashionable when it comes to dressing himself, but he wouldn't be caught dead without the perfect accessory: a curved blade attached to a long, wooden handle. It's called a scythe.

In 1957, the Grim Reaper (above, left) sat down to a high-stakes game of chess in the foreign film *The Seventh Seal*. Chess not your game? If the Grim Reaper ever comes knocking on your door, invite him to play *Halo* or *Super Mario Brothers* instead. Old folks are never very good at video games, and thanks to Konami's *Death Jr.* series (right), you can even try beating the Grim Reaper at his own game.

FUNNY BONES

An 1825 gravestone in Cooperstown, New York, bears the following inscription: *Lord, she is thin!* The stonecutter didn't intend to comment on Mrs. Susannah Ensign's weight. He meant to write the word *thine* (meaning "yours"), but ran out of space.

Americans spend more than $13 billion on funerals every year. One big trend in this alive-and-kicking industry: Funerals are becoming more and more personalized. For example, at the 2003 funeral of a Massachusetts ice-cream vendor, mourners lined up at an ice-cream truck to get free Popsicles.

Rest your tired bones in the Sedlec Ossuary and your bones won't be alone. Located in the Czech Republic, the chapel contains approximately 40,000 human skeletons . . . as wall and furniture decorations!

Six hundred thousand buttons might sound like a lot of buttons, but that's how many it takes to cover an entire hearse. Just ask Dalton Stevens, the man known as "The Button King." His rainbow-colored hearse—which also contains a button-covered coffin—is on display at the Button Museum in Bishopville, South Carolina.

FOUL PLAY

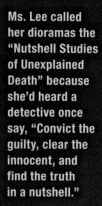

A gruesome *grandma*? Believe it, death-heads.

Her name was Frances Glessner Lee, and she was guilty of many murderous acts during the 1940s. Nonetheless, police officers were among her biggest fans. The reason: Ms. Lee's only victims were dolls; her only crime scenes were contained inside dollhouses; and her only motive was to educate new recruits about the art of crime-solving.

Ms. Lee came from a wealthy family and didn't need to work, but being a volunteer police officer didn't feel like work to her. She had a keen talent for observation, and she believed it was a talent that could be taught. After befriending a professional medical examiner near her estate in New Hampshire, Ms. Glessner became increasingly interested in criminology, the study of crime and criminals. Professors in that field became equally interested in meeting Ms. Glessner when she thought up the idea of creating ultra-realistic—yet ultra-tiny—murder scenes. Each diorama was a mystery based on one or more actual police cases, and observers were to solve the mystery by analyzing the microevidence left behind.

With nimble fingers and a flair for decorating—some yellow wallpaper here, some blood splats there—Ms. Lee combined criminology and miniature-making in uncanny ways. She was so detail-oriented that she knitted her own mini stockings, and even though one mini wall calendar was open only to April, it also concealed pages for each remaining month of the year!

Ms. Lee passed away in 1962, but her tiny acts of murder are still used as teaching tools today.

HISTOIRE NATURELLE DES MOLLUSQUES

PIERRE DENYS DE MONTFORT

1802

Property of E.H.

ACTUAL SIZE!

After filing the above report with ENCYCLOPEDIA HORRIFICA, Joshua Gee strangely began building a miniature version of his office at horrific headquarters. It is believed that Investigator Gee hoped to feature a tribute to the Nutshell Studies on the next page. Alas, nobody can say for certain, because mystery has an eerie way of finding the office of Investigator Gee—even an office rendered in one-twelfth the normal size....

ROSWELL

UFO?

THE CHIEF IS MISSING!

BULLETS (SILVER)

I'LL BE RIGHT BACK! —JG

I WANT TO BELIEVE

"I lost audio contact with the Chief around midnight," says the Mysterious Mister Grutty of the night Joshua Gee disappeared. "He was found lying on his office floor. No hat, no headset, and no pulse..."

The Mysterious Mister Grutty left the room to summon help. When he returned, the corpse was gone—as if it had gotten up and walked away!

Nobody at horrific headquarters is certain who might wish to harm Investigator Gee, but everybody has theories. Some say his miniature office (pictured) contains clues pointing to one of the villains featured in an earlier chapter. Analyze the crime scene using your knowledge of all things ghoulish and ghastly, and be sure to examine Investigator Gee's research journal, too. Select pages appear in the front and back of this book.

ENCYCLOPEDIA HORRIFICA is counting on you, fear seekers.

Selected Bibliography

Complete reference list available at www.joshuagee.com.

DRACULA LIVES!

Barber, Paul. "Staking Claims: The Vampires of Folklore and Fiction." *Skeptical Inquirer*, March/April 1996, http://www.csicop.org/si/9603/staking.html

Bram Stoker's "Dracula": A Centennial Exhibition at the Rosenbach Museum & Library. Philadelphia: Rosenbach Museum & Library, 1997.

Dickson, Seth. "Vampires Uncloaked." *Bizarre* magazine, May/June 1997.

Eddy, Beverley D., ed. *Dracula: A Translation of the 1488 Nürnberg Edition*. Philadelphia: Rosenbach Museum & Library, 1985.

Garden, Nancy. *Vampires*. New York: J. B. Lippincott Company, 1973.

Guiley, Rosemary Ellen. *The Encyclopedia of Vampires, Werewolves, and Other Monsters*. New York: Checkmark Books, 2005.

McNally, Raymond T., and Radu Florescu. *In Search of Dracula: The History of Dracula and Vampires*, rev. ed. New York: Houghton Mifflin Company, 1994.

Melton, J. Gordon, ed. "Dracula, The Text." *All Things Dracula: A Bibliography of Editions, Reprints, Adaptations, and Translations of Dracula*. http://www.cesnur.org/2003/dracula/ (accessed on July 16, 2006).

Summers, Montague. *The Vampire: His Kith and Kin*. London: Trubner & Company, 1928.

Washburn, Michael. "Bloody Good: How a Cruel 15th-Century Ruler Morphed into the Monster We Love Today." *Philadelphia City Paper*, Oct. 27, 2005, http://www.citypaper.net/articles/2005-10-27/art.shtml

Williams, Daniel. "Romania Takes Its Stake in the Dracula Legend To Heart." *Washington Post*, Dec. 1, 2004.

IT CAME FROM THE SEA!

Blythe, Richard. *Dragons and Other Fabulous Beasts*. New York: Grosset & Dunlap, 1977.

Bondeson, Jan. "The Feejee Mermaid." Chap. 3 in *The Feejee Mermaid and Other Essays in Natural and Unnatural History*. Ithaca, NY: Cornell University Press, 1999.

Coleman, Lauren, and Jerome Clark. *Cryptozoology A to Z*. New York: Fireside Books, 1999.

Columbus, Christopher. *The Journal of Christopher Columbus*. London: Hakluyt Society, 1893. Reprint, Boston: Adamant Media, 2005.

Ellis, Richard. *The Search for the Giant Squid*. New York: Lyons Press, 1998.

Fernicola, Richard G. *Twelve Days of Terror: A Definitive Investigation of the 1916 New Jersey Shark Attacks*. New York: Lyons Press, 2001.

Morelle, Rebecca. "Giant Squid Grabs London Audience." *BBC News Online*, Feb. 28, 2006. http://news.bbc.co.uk/2/hi/science/nature/4756514.stm

O'Shea, Steve. "Estimating Age and Growth Rate in 'Architeuthis dux.'" *Octopus News Magazine Online*. http://www.tonmo.com/science/public/architeuthis-age.php (accessed on July 24, 2006).

Time-Life Books. *Mysterious Creatures*. Mysteries of the Unknown. Richmond, VA: Time-Life Books Inc., 1988.

ALIEN INVASION!

Arnold, Kenneth. "I Did See the Flying Disks!" *FATE* magazine, Spring 1948.

Associated Press. "Flier Dies Chasing a 'Flying Saucer.'" *New York Times*, Jan. 9, 1948.

Clark, Jerome. *The UFO Book: Encyclopedia of the Extraterrestrial*. Detroit: Visible Ink Press, 1998.

Deardorff, J., B. Haisch, B. Maccabee, and H. E. Puthoff. "Inflation-Theory Implications for Extraterrestrial Visitation." *Journal of the British Interplanetary Society*, vol. 58 (Jan./Feb. 2005): 43–50.

Haydon, S. E. "A Windmill Demolishes It." *Dallas Morning News*, April 17, 1897.

Korff, Kal K. *The Roswell UFO Crash: What They Don't Want You to Know*. New York: Dell Publishing, 2000.

McAndrew, James. *The Roswell Report: Case Closed*. Washington, D.C.: U.S. Government Printing Office, 1997.

Randle, Kevin. *Project Blue Book Exposed*. New York: Marlowe & Company, 1997.

Schumach, Murray. "'Disk' Near Bomb Test Site Is Just a Weather Balloon." *New York Times*, July 9, 1947.

Shaffer, Josh. "Flying Saucer Tale Is Serious Business in Small Texas Town." *Fort Worth Star Telegram*, August 29, 2002.

Shostak, Seth. "Interstellar Signal from the 70s Continues to Puzzle Researchers." *Space.com*, Dec. 5, 2002. http://www.space.com/searchforlife/seti_shostak_wow_021205.html

Shuch, H. Paul. "SETI Sensitivity: Calibrating on a Wow! Signal." *SETI League*. http://www.setileague.org/articles/calibwow.htm

Time-Life Books. *Alien Encounters*. Mysteries of the Unknown. Richmond, VA: Time-Life Books Inc., 1992.

Time-Life Books. *The UFO Phenomenon*. Mysteries of the Unknown. Richmond, VA: Time-Life Books Inc., 1987.

HOWLING AT THE MOON!

Aylesworth, Thomas G. *The Story of Werewolves*. New York: McGraw-Hill, 1978.

Baring-Gould, Sabine. *The Book of Were-Wolves*. 1865. Reprint, Mineola, NY: Dover, 2006.

Britt, Robert Roy. "Full Moon and Lunatic Dogs." *Space.com*, Jan. 9, 2001. http://www.space.com/scienceastronomy/solarsystem/lunatic_dogs_010109-1.html

Garden, Nancy. *Werewolves*. New York: Bantam Books, 1973.

Guiley, Rosemary Ellen. (See "Dracula Lives!")

McHargue, Georgess. *Meet the Werewolf*. Philadelphia: J. B. Lippincott Company, 1976.

Myring, Lynn. *Vampires, Werewolves & Demons*. Supernatural Guides. London: Usborne, 1990.

Orenstein, Catherine. *Little Red Riding Hood Uncloaked*. New York: Basic Books, 2002.

Pourcher, Abbé Pierre. *The Beast of Gévaudan*. 1889. Translated by Derek Brockis. Bloomington, Indiana: Author House, 2006.

Ralston, W. E. S. *The Songs of the Russian People, as Illustrative of Slavonic Mythology and Russian Social Life*. London: Ellis & Green, 1872.

Roach, John. "Full Moon Affect on Behavior Minimal, Studies Say." *National Geographic News*, Feb. 6, 2004. http://news.nationalgeographic.com/news/2002/12/1218_021218_moon.html

Steiger, Brad. *The Werewolf Book: The Encyclopedia of Shape-Shifting Beings*. Detroit: Visible Ink Press, 1999.

Thompson, Richard H. *Wolf-Hunting in France in the Reign of Louis XV*. Lewiston, NY: Edwin Mellen Press, 1991.

Townley, John. "Can the Full Moon Affect Human Behavior?" *Inner Self*. http://www.innerself.com/Astrology/full_moon.htm (accessed on August 8, 2006).

"THAT'S THE SPIRIT!"

An American Haunting. DVD. Directed by Courtney Solomon. 2005. Santa Monica, CA: Lionsgate Home Entertainment, 2006.

Auerbach, Loyd. "On Photos of Ghosts and Orbs." *The Paranormal Network*, 2005. http://www.mindreader.com/Photos/index.htm

Bord, Janet and Colin. *The World of the Unexplained*. London: Blandford, 1998.

Chéroux, Clément, Andreas Fischer, Pierre Apraxine, Denis Canguilhem, and Sophie Schmit. *The Perfect Medium*. New Haven, CT: Yale University Press, 2004.

The Donnelly Family [pseud.]. 2006. Interviews by Joshua Gee. Tape recordings. Sept. 2–3. Dutchess County, NY. Actual names withheld by mutual agreement.

Fitzhugh, Pat. *The Bell Witch: The Full Account*. Nashville, TN: Armand Press, 2000.

Floyd, E. Randall. *In the Realm of Ghosts and Hauntings*. New York: Barnes & Noble Books, 2006.

Goddard, Victor. *Flight Towards Reality*. London: Turnstone Books, 1975.

Guiley, Rosemary Ellen. *The Encyclopedia of Ghosts and Spirits*. New York: Checkmark Books, 2000.

Hendrix, Grady. Review of *An American Haunting*. Directed by Courtney Solomon. *Slate*. May 4, 2006. http://www.slate.com/id/2141069/

Herdman Ackley, Helen. "Our Haunted House on the Hudson." *Reader's Digest*, May 1977.

Hyde, Deborah, and Karl Derrick. "Portenders of Death: Black Dogs." *Unnatural Predators*. http://www.arkanefx.com/unpred/portender/bdog.html (accessed on Sept. 28, 2006).

Ingram, M. V. *Authenticated History of the Bell Witch*. 1894. A facsimile of the first edition. Union City, TN: Pioneer Press, 2000.

Kaczmarek, Dale, and Matt Hucke. "Ghost Photographs." *Ghost Research Society*. http://www.ghostresearch.org/ghostpics/ (accessed on Sept. 20, 2006).

Kavanagh, Mark. "The Ghost of Nyack." *Kavanagh Family Home Page*. March 6, 2005. http://home.comcast.net/~subwaymark/Ghost/ghost.htm

Kugel, Herb. "The Air Marshall and the Unexplained." *FATE* magazine, July 2000, 10.

Middle Tennessee Skeptics. "The Bell Witch Project." *MTS Online*. http://mtskeptics.homestead.com/BellWitch.html (accessed Oct. 16, 2006).

Nickell, Joe. "Ghostly Photos." Chap. 18 in *Real-Life X-Files: Investigating the Paranormal*. Lexington, KY: University Press of Kentucky, 2001.

Norder, Dan. "The Face in the Mirror." *MythologyWeb*. http://www.mythologyweb.com/bloodymary.html (accessed on Sept. 9, 2006).

Parkinson, Danny J., and Ian Topham. "The Brown Lady of Raynham Hall." *Ghosts and Hauntings in Britain*. http://www.mysteriousbritain.co.uk/hauntings/brownlady.html (accessed on Sept. 26, 2006).

Parkinson, Danny J., and Ian Topham. "Phantom Dogs." *Ghosts and Hauntings in Britain*. http://www.mysteriousbritain.co.uk/folklore/black_dogs.html (accessed on Sept. 28, 2006).

Ratliff, John R. "Never Open E-Mails from Dead Girls." *BreakTheChain.org*, July 14, 2004. http://www.breakthechain.org/exclusives/deadgirl.html

Reeve, Christopher. "The Black Dog of Bungay: A Brief History." *Bungay Suffolk Town Guide*. http://www.bungay-suffolk.co.uk/history/black-dog.htm (accessed on Oct. 1, 2006).

Robertson County Archives, Springfield, TN. "John Bell Deed." Will/Estate Settlement Book 3: 227–228.

Steiger, Brad. *Real Ghosts, Restless Spirits, and Haunted Places*. Detroit: Visible Ink Press, 2003.

Time-Life Books. *Hauntings*. Mysteries of the Unknown. Richmond, VA: Time-Life Books Inc., 1989.

Time-Life Books. *Phantom Encounters*. Mysteries of the Unknown. Richmond, VA: Time-Life Books Inc., 1988.

Wagner, Stephen. "The Best Ghost Photos Ever Taken." *About.com: Paranormal Phenomena*. http://paranormal.about.com/library/weekly/aa101402a.htm (accessed on August 18, 2006).

Williams, Docia. "The Brown Lady of Raynham Hall." In *Haunted Encounters: Real-Life Stories of Supernatural Experiences*, edited by Ginnie Siena Bivona, Dorothy McConachie, and Mitchel Whitington, 37–43. Dallas, TX: Atriad Press, 2003.

AMAZING BRAIN WAVES!

Chéroux, Clément, Andreas Fischer, Pierre Apraxine, Denis Canguilhem, and Sophie Schmit. (*See* "That's the Spirit!")

Central Intelligence Agency (CIA). "Ministry to Study Psychic Powers, UFOs for Future Industry." CIA, Feb. 19, 1993. Now declassified and available online at http://www.foia.cia.gov/.

Defense Intelligence Agency (DIA). *Soviet and Czechoslovakian Parapsychology Research*. Washington, DC: DIA, 1975. Now declassified and available online at http://www.dia.mil/publicaffairs/Foia/foia.htm

Fulford, Benjamin. "Sony Sees Sense to Discontinue ESP Research." *South China Morning Post*, July 7, 1998.

Huyghe, Patrick. "Closing the Dream Factory." *Fortean Times*, Oct. 1998.

Kotler, Steven. "ESP: Extra Sony Perception." *Wired* magazine, Sept. 1996.

McMoneagle, Joseph. *The Stargate Chronicles: Memoirs of a Psychic Spy*. Charlottesville, VA: Hampton Roads, 2002.

Piazza, Judyth. "The CIA's Operation Stargate: Remote Viewing and Mind Control." *Calder Gazette*, August 18, 2004.

Radin, Dean. *Entangled Minds: Extrasensory Experiences in a Quantum Reality.* New York, NY: Paraview/Pocket Books, 2006.

Smith, Paul H. "How to Do a Simple Remote Viewing Session." *Remote Viewing Instructional Services.* http://www.rviewer.com/ SimpleRemoteViewing.html (accessed Sept. 18, 2006).

Time-Life Books. *Psychic Powers.* Mysteries of the Unknown. Richmond, VA: Time-Life Books Inc., 1987.

THE BLACK CAT'S PATH!

Answers Corporation. "Phobias, Compiled by Answers Corp." *Answers.com.* http://www.answers.com/library/Phobias (accessed on Dec. 6, 2006).

Borgos, Eric. "The Largest List of Superstitions on the Web." *Superstitions Database.* http://www.oldsuperstitions.com (accessed Oct. 12, 2006).

Culbertson, Fredd. "The Phobia List." *The Phobia List.* http://www. phobialist.com (accessed Dec. 6, 2006).

Pickering, David. *Cassell's Dictionary of Superstitions.* 1995. Reprint, New York, NY: Sterling Publishing, 2002.

Warner, Marina. *No Go the Bogeyman: Scaring, Lulling & Making Mock.* New York, NY: Farrar, Straus and Giroux, 1998.

THE FORBIDDEN BOOKSHELF!

Budge, E. A. Wallis. *The Book of the Dead: The Chapters of Coming Forth by Day.* 1898. A facsimile of the first edition. Boston: Adamant Media, 2001.

Lovecraft, H. P. "History of the Necronomicon." In *The Necronomicon Files: The Truth Behind the Legend.* Edited by Daniel Harms and John Wisdom Gonce III, 303–306. Boston: Weiser Books, 2003.

TO BE OR NOT ZOMBIE!

Ackermann, Hans-W., and Jeanine Gauthier. "The Ways and Nature of the Zombi." *Journal of American Folklore,* vol. 104 (1991): 466–494.

Kruszelnicki, Karl. "Zombies." In *Great Mythconceptions: The Science Behind the Myths.* Kansas City, MO: Andrews McMeel Publishing, 2006.

Wallis, Claudia. "Zombies: Do They Exist?" *Time* magazine, Oct. 17, 1983.

Wilson, Tracy V. "How Zombies Work." *How Stuff Works.* http:// science.howstuffworks.com/zombie.htm (accessed on Nov. 7, 2006).

TRICKED BY PIXIES!

Boese, Alex. "The Top 100 April Fool's Day Hoaxes of All Time." *Museum of Hoaxes.* http://www.museumofhoaxes.com/hoax/ aprilfool/index (accessed on Jan. 19, 2007).

Bord, Janet and Colin. (*See* "That's the Spirit!")

The Cottingley Network. "Cottingley Fairies." *Cottingley.Net: The Cottingley Network.* http://www.cottingley.net/fairies.shtml (accessed on Jan. 24, 2007).

Doyle, A. Conan. "The Evidence for Fairies." *The Strand Magazine,* March 1921.

Doyle, A. Conan. "Fairies Photographed: An Epoch-Making Event." *The Strand Magazine,* Dec. 1920.

Ezard, John. "Fake Dragon Rakes in Deal for Author." *Guardian UK News,* March 29, 2004. http://www.guardian.co.uk

Folger, Tim. "Hotheads." *Discover* magazine, April 1995.

Froud, Brian, and Alan Lee. *Faeries.* New York: Harry N. Abrams, 1978.

New York Times. "Radio Listeners in Panic, Taking War Drama as Fact." Oct. 31, 1938.

Randi, James. "The Case of the Cottingley Fairies." *James Randi Educational Foundation.* http://www.randi.org/library/cottingley/ index.html (accessed on Jan. 24, 2007).

Sturleson, Snorre. *The Younger Eddas of Snorre Sturleson.* Translated by I. A. Blackwell. London: Norroena Society, 1906. http://www. gutenberg.org/files/14726/14726-h/14726-h.htm

THE CURSE OF THE MUMMY!

Barlow, Bart. "A Lost Town Populated by Legends." *New York Times,* Oct. 26, 1980.

Carter, Howard, and A. C. Mace. *The Discovery of the Tomb of Tutankhamen.* 1923. Reprint, New York: Dover, 1977.

Corelli, Marie. "Warned Carnarvon of Peril in Tomb, Says Marie Corelli." *New York World,* March 24, 1923.

Handwerk, Brian. "Egypt's 'King Tut Curse' Caused by Tomb Toxins?" *National Geographic News,* May 6, 2005. http://news.nationalgeo- graphic.com/news/2005/05 /0510_050506_tvcurse.html

Kruszelnicki, Karl. "Curse of King Tut." In *Great Mythconceptions: The Science Behind the Myths.* Kansas City, MO: Andrews McMeel Publishing, 2006.

New York Times. "Carnarvon's Death Spreads Theories About Vengeance." April 6, 1923.

New York Times. "Curse of Pharaoh Denied by Winlock." Jan. 26, 1934.

Nelson, Mark R. "The Mummy's Curse: Historical Cohort Study." *British Medical Journal,* vol. 325 (Dec. 21–28, 2002): 1482– 1484.

Nickell, Joe. "The Kennedy Curse." Chap. 9 in *Real-Life X-Files: Investigating the Paranormal.* Lexington, KY: University Press of Kentucky, 2001.

Patch, Susanne Steinem. *Blue Mystery: The Story of the Hope Diamond.* Washington, DC: Smithsonian Institution Press, 1976.

Reeves, Nicholas. *Into the Mummy's Tomb.* New York: Scholastic, 1992.

Rierden, Andi. "Dudleytown: A Hamlet That Can't Get Rid of Its Ghosts." *New York Times,* Oct. 29, 1989.

Winkler, Robert. "Old Curse Haunts New England Forest." *National Geographic News,* Oct. 30, 2002. http://news.nationalgeographic. com/news/2002/10/1030_021030_BirdersJournal.html

GRUESOME GOOD-BYES!

Botz, Corinne May. *The Nutshell Studies of Unexplained Death.* New York: Monacelli Press, 2004.

Kahn, Eve. "Murder is Merely Child's Play." *San Francisco Chronicle Online,* Oct. 20, 2004. http://www.sfgate.com/.

Miller, Laura J. "Frances Glessner Lee: Brief Life of a Miniaturist, 1878–1962." *Harvard Magazine,* Sept.–Oct. 2005.

US Census Bureau. "World Vital Events Per Time Unit: 2007." *International Data Base.* http://www.census.gov (accessed on Jan. 28, 2007).

Index

A

Aborigines, 120
Acacia constricta (white thorn), 4
Ackley, Cynthia, aka Kavanagh, 42, 43
Ackley, Helen, 42
Albert Schweitzer Hospital, 108
Alexander the Great, 21
Alexander, Shaun, 122
alien
   abduction, 25
   close encounters, 21–22, 24–27
   time line, 20–27
alien–human hybrids, 27
Amenti, Neva Ankhasa, 66
American Magazine, The, 47
American Medical Association, 124
anti-zombification law, 109
apparitions, definition of, 45
Archie the *Architeuthis dux* (giant squid), 12
Area 51, Nevada, 23
Arnold, Kenneth, 21, 23, 104
artifact spirit (*tsukumogami*), 40
Artist's Handbook of Materials and Techniques,
   The, 119
Aspergillus flavus, 119
Auerbach, Loyd "Professor Paranormal," 38,
   44–45, 60, 104; books by, 44
Authenticated History of the Bell Witch, An, 37

B

Bacon, Sir Francis, 70
banshees, 6, 112
Barnum Museum, the, 17, 18
Barnum, P. T., 17–18, 137
Barsanti, Michael, 5
Bast, 67
bat (vampire), 7
bean-nighe (banshees), 112
Beast of Gévaudan, the, 28, 30–32
Bell Witch Cave, 38
Bell Witch, 36–38, 39
Bell, Betsy, 36–38
Bell, John, 36–38
Bell, Lucy, 36
berserkir, 29
bishop-fish, 19
Black Dog (hound), 36, 68
Bloody Mary ghost, 39
Blythburgh Church, 68
Bogeymen, 90–91, 124
"Book of Going Forth by Day, The," 103
"Book of the Dead, The," 103
Book of Were-Wolves, The, 28
Boston Red Sox, 122
Boulet, Jeanne, 30
Bradbury, Ray, 100
Brazel, William "Mac," 24
Bridge Café, 75
British Civil Aviation Authority, 26

Brooks, Max, 107
Brown Lady of Raynham Hall, The, 45, 58–59,
   60, 96
Brown, James, 8
Buffy the Vampire Slayer, 4, 50

C

"Call of Cthulhu, The," 103
cane toad (*Bufo marinus*), 110
Cardiff Giant, the, 17, 135
Carnarvon, Lord, 118
Carter, Howard, 118
cats, 66–67, 97
Cemetery of Dogs (Cimetière des Chiens), 70
Chaney, Lon, 31
Chastel, Jean, 31
Chicago Cubs, 122
Chinnery, Mrs. Mabel, 137
Cimetière des Chiens (Cemetery of Dogs), 70
clairvoyance, definition of, 82
Columbus, Christopher, 19
Coney Island Circus Sideshow, Coney Island
   USA, 17
Corelli, Marie, 118
Corpse Bride, 78
Country Life magazine, 58, 60
Courtney, James, 16
Crane-Phillips House, 137
crime solving, 127
crop circles, 22
Croft, Lara, 119
Croquemitaine, Monsieur and Madame ("Mr.
   and Mrs. Mitten-Biter"), 90
Cthulhu of the Old Ones, 102–103
Curse of the Bambino, 122
Curse of the Billy Goat, 122
Cycle of the Werewolf, 100

D

Daedalus, HMS, 137
Dallas Morning News, 26
datura plant, 109, 110
Davis, Wade, 110–111
Day of the Dead (*Día de los Muertos*), 124
de Montfort, Pierre Dénys, 11, 127
Death, 124–125
Death Jr. video game series, 125
Demodex mites, 117
Dennis, Glenn, 24
Día de los Muertos (Day of the Dead), 124
Discover magazine, 116
Donnelly family, 49–57
Doyle, Sir Arthur Conan, 61, 114
"Dracole Waida," 6
Dracula, 2, 3, 5, 7, 100
Dracula 3000, 7
Dracula, Count, 2, 4, 7, 112
Dracula Festival, 5
draculin, 7

dragon, 116
Dreamland, Nevada, 23
Dudley, Abiel and Barzillai, 123
Dudleytown, 123
"Dunwich Horror, The," 100, 103

E

Easter Island, 21
ectoplasm, 61, 62
ectoplasmic spiral, 65, 137
Edison, Thomas, 47
Electronic Voice Phenomena (EVP), 55
Elfman, Danny, 78
Elves, Dark and Light, 112
Enkidu, 29
Ennemoser, Dr. Joseph, 8
Ensign, Mrs. Susannah, 126
Evans, Arthur, 34
evil eye amulet (*nazar boncuğu*), 120
Evolution Store, The, 76–77
extrasensory perception (ESP), 44, 85, 86,
   87, 88

F

faeries, 6, 112–115
Fairly OddParents, The, 51
fairy rings, 113
Fate magazine, 104
fearology, 90
Feejee Mermaid, 17–18
ferret, ghost, 69
Flying Dutchman, 16
flying saucers, 21, 23, 24
Flight Towards Reality, 137
forest, cursed, 123
Fortune Teller, The, 78
Frankenstein Meets the Wolf Man, 31
Frankenstein, 100
Frankenstein's monster, 31
Franklin Institute Science Museum, 116
Friday the 13th, 93, 94, 95, 97
fugu sashimi, 111
funerals, personalized, 126

G

Garnier, Gilles, 30
geocaching, 74
George IV, King of England, 60
Gévaudan, France, 30–32 (*see also* Beast of)
ghosts
   expert on, 44–45
   haunting, 36–43, 45
   photos, 16, 58, 61–65
ghost hunting, 46–52, 54–57, eight stages of,
   50
Ghostbusters, 46
giant squid (*Architeuthis dux*), 10, 12, 13
globsters, 10
Gonsalvus, Petrus, 33

Goddard, Sir Victor, 137
Great Bambino (Babe Ruth), 122
Great Pyramid of Egypt, 21
Grenier, Jean, 30
Griffiths, Frances, 114–115
Grim Reaper, 125
Groom Lake, Nevada, 23

H

Haitian Penal Code Article 246, 109
Hannum, David, 135
Hartsdale Pet Cemetery, 70
Harvard Peabody Museum, 18
*Haunted Encounters: Real-life Stories of
    Supernatural Experiences*, 60
Hawaiian Volcanoes National Park, 120
Haydon, S. E., 26
hematophagy, 7
Histoire Naturelle des Mollusques, 11, 127
"History of *The Necronomicon*," 103
hoaxes, 22, 26, 34, 37, 58, 62, 63–65, 80, 112,
    114, 116, 137
Hobbit-man (*Homo floresiensis*), 34
Hoffman, E. T. A., 100
Hollidge, Alfred, 67
Holmes, Sherlock, 114
Hope Diamond, 121
Hound of the Baskervilles, The, 68
"House on Haunted Hill, The," 100
hypertrichosis universalis, 33

I

Ibuka, Masaru, 87
Ingram, Martin Van Buren, 37
International Thylacine Specimen Database
    (ITSD), 32

J

Jackson, Andrew, 38
Jackson, Freddy, 64, 137
Jackson, Shirley, 100
Jaws, 15
Jekyll & Hyde Club, 75
Jones, Indiana, 119
*Journal of the British Interplanetary Society,
    The*, 27
Jumbo the Elephant, 17, 135
Jurassic Park, 32

K

Kavanagh, Cynthia, aka Ackley, 42, 43
King, Stephen, 70, 100
Kraken, the, 10–13
Krueger, Freddy, 91
Kubodera, Tsunemi, 12

L

Lee, Frances Glessner, 127
Leiber, Arnold, 33
Leidenfrost effect, 110
Little Mermaid, The, 17

Loft, Captain Bob, 41
Loftus, Colonel, 60
Lord of the Rings, The, 34
loup-garou, 30
Lovecraft, H. P., 100, 102, 103
Lowell, Percival, 22
Lugosi, Bela, 3
lunacy, origins of word, 33
*Lunar Effect, The: Biological Tides and Human
    Emotions*, 33
Luster, John and Jenny, 54
lycanthropes, or lycans, 29
lycanthropy, definitions of, 28, 29, 30
Lycaon, 29, 34

M

Madden Curse, 122
manatee, 19
Man-Eating Chicken, 17, 135
Mantell, Captain Thomas, Jr., 27
Marryat, Captain Frederick, 60
Mars and Its Canals, 22
Mary I , Queen of England, 39
Matawan Man-Eater, 15
Mathews, Eddie, 122
Matrix, The, 83
Maxwell, Greg Sheldon, 137
McNear, Tom, 85
Meehan, Michael, 16
mercreatures/merpeople, 18–19
merrows, 6
Metronoma, 102
mind reading (telepathy), 83, 88
Minotaur, 34
mites, 117
Mitten-Biter, Mr. and Mrs. (Monsieur and
    Madame Croquemitaine), 90
monk-fish, 19

N

Narcisse, Clairvius, 108
National Aviation Reporting Center on
    Anomalous Phenomena, 27
National Museum of Natural History,
    Washington, DC, 121
Natural History Museum, London, 12
nazar boncuğu (evil eye amulet), 120
Necronomicon, The, 102–103
New York State Supreme Court, 42
New York Sun, The, 22, 34
New York World, The, 8, 118
Night of the Living Dead, 106
Nightmare Before Christmas, The, 78
Nightmare on Elm Street, A, 91
Nosferatu: A Symphony of Horror, 3, 9
Nutshell Studies of Unexplained Death,
    127

O

O'Rahilly, Tony, 137
Oxenby manor house, 67

P

panspermia, 20
Paole, Arnald, 8
Paranormal Investigation of NYC, 49–51
paranormal, definition of, 44
Pele, 120
Pet Sematary (novel), 70
"Pet Sematary" (song lyrics), 70
Peterson, Professor Rolf, 32, 33
phobias, definitions of, 90, 91, 93, 95, 97, 99
phookas, 6
pickled dragon, 116
Pirates of the Caribbean, 11, 16
"Pit and the Pendulum, The," 100
Poe, Edgar Allan, 100
pointing the bone, 120
Polidori, Dr. John William, 100
poltergeist, 38, 57; definition of, 45
Poltergeist, 45
Popular Astronomy, 22
Potter, Harry, 102
Pourcher, Abbé, 30
precognition, definition of, 84
Price, Harry, 47, 59
Project Blue Book, 24
Project ESPER (ExtraSensory Perception and
    Excitation Research), 87
Project Mogul, 24
Project Star Gate, 81–86
Provand, Captain, 58, 59
Pseudomonas, 119
psychic, *see* ESP
puffer fish, 111
"Punch and Judy" show, 91
Punch, Mr., 91
puppets, 78–79
Puthoff, Dr. Harold, 83

Q

Quirk, John, 41

R

rabies, 32
Radu the Handsome, 3
Railroad Stories magazine, 41
Ralston, W. R. S., 28
Ramey, Major General Roger, 24
Ramones, the, 70
"Raven, The," 100
Raynham Hall, *see* Brown Lady
*Reading the Enemy's Mind: Inside Star Gate,
    America's Psychic Espionage Program*, 82
Reid, Yolanda, 36, 37
remote viewing, controlled, 83; definition of, 82
Repo, Don, 41
Rhine, Dr. J. B., 88
Robertson County (Tennessee) Archives, 36
Robin, Henri, 61
Romero, George A., 106
Rose, Deb, 17
Rosenbach Museum and Library, 5, 6

Roswell Army Air Field (RAAF), 24
Roswell Daily Record, 24
Roswell, New Mexico, 23, 24, 25
Ruth, Babe (Great Bambino), 122

S

Sako, Yoichiro, 87
Sand-Man, The, 100
Sanko, Erik, 78–79
Schreck, Max, 9
scythe, 125
sea monster, 11–12
séance, 58, 61
Sedlec Ossuary, 126
Serpent and the Rainbow, The, 110
SETI (Search for Extraterrestrial Intelligence), 26
Seventh Seal, The, 125
shape-shifters, 28
shark
    great white, 15
    megalodon, 14
    speckled carpet, 14
Shelley, Mary, 100
Shira, Indres, 58, 59
Sianis, Billy, 122
simulacra, 62
Skeleton Key (band), 78
Smith, Paul H., 82–86
Smith, Will, 86
Snagov Lake, 2
Society for Research on Rapport and
    Telekinesis, The (SORRAT), 80
Something Wicked This Way Comes, 100
Songs of the Russian People, 28
South China Morning Post, 87
sperm whale, 10, 13
Spielberg, Steven, 15
Sports Illustrated Cover Jinx, 122
Stambovsky, Jeffrey, 42
Staphylococcus, 119
Star Wars, 26, 80, 102
Stark, USS, 84
Stevens, Dalton, the Button King, 126
Stevenson, Robert Louis, 75
Stoker, Bram, 2, 5–7
Stone, Lucia, 60
Strand Magazine, The, 114
Strange Case of Dr. Jekyll and Mr. Hyde, The, 75
Sturges, Daniel "Dan," 49–57
Summers, Buffy, 4
Summers, Montague, 4
superstition, 8, 90, 92–93, 94–99, 118
survival horror video games, 107

T

tapetum lucidum, 67
Targoviste Palace, 3
Tasmanian wolf (thylacine), 32
taxidermy, 69

telekinesis, definition of, 80
telepathy (mind reading), 83; definition of, 88
"Tell-Tale Heart, The," 100
Tennessee Historical Commission, 38
tetrodotoxin, 111
Thayer's Historic Bed 'n' Breakfast, 66
thylacine (Tasmanian wolf), 32
Time magazine, 108
Tolkien, J. R. R., 34
tomb raiders, 118–119
Tom Thumb the Dwarf Elephant, 17, 135
Townshend, Marquess Charles "Turnip," and
    Lady, 59, 60; *see also* Brown Lady
Tracy, Captain Keith, 16
Travels of Sir John Mandeville, The, 116
Trent, Paul, 21
Trewella, Mathew, 19
tsukumogami (artifact spirit), 40
Turck, Sven, 80
Tut, King, 118

U

ufologists, 20, 21, 23, 24, 26, 27
umibōzu, 19
Unidentified Aerial Phenomena (UAP), 27
Unidentified Flying Objects (UFOs), 20–27,
    naming of, 24
U.S. Air Force, 21, 22, 24
U.S. Army, 85
U.S. Coast Guard, 15

V

Valuckas, Jonathan, 102–103
vampires, 4, 5, 8–9
Vampire Killing Kit, 9
Vampire, The: His Kith and Kin, 4
Vampyre, The, 100
van der Decken, Captain Hendrik, 16
Van Helsing, Abraham, 3
Villella, Dominick "Dom," 49–57, 69

Vlad III, Prince of Wallachia, 2
Voivode (Warrior Prince), 3

W

Walpole, Lady Dorothy, 60; *see also* Brown
    Lady
Walton, Travis, 25
War of the Worlds, The, 23, 116
Warfel, Jennifer, 50–57
Warrior Prince (*Voivode*), 3
Watertown, S.S., 16, 62
Washington Square Park, 74–75
Wells, H. G., 116
werewolf, 28–33
    French, 29–30
    Hollywood, 31
white thorn (*Acacia constricta*), 4
Williams, Docia Schultz, 60
Willowby House, 50, 56
Wise County (Texas) Historical Commission, 26
Wolf-Man, The, 29, 31
wolfsbane, 31
World War Z, 107
Wright, Elsie, 114–115

XY

X-Files, The, 27
X-Men, 81

Z

Zamora, Lonnie, 22, 24
Zener cards, 78–79; 88
Zennor Church, 19
Zigun, Dick, 17
Zoltan: Hound of Dracula, 7
Zombie Survival Guide, The, 107
zombi, 108–111
zombies, 106–107
Zombies Ate My Neighbors video game, 107
Zozobra, 91

ANSWERS TO "THE BEASTS OF BARNUM" ON PAGE 17

A. HUMBUG! Customers paid to see a large block of stone carved to look like a fossilized "giant." In response to this, a banker named David Hannum is said to have made the famous remark, "There's a sucker born every minute."

B. REAL! Jumbo the Elephant weighed 14,000 pounds and measured twelve feet tall. Because of him, the English language now includes the word *jumbo* (meaning "uncommonly large").

C. REAL! Tom Thumb the Dwarf Elephant made Jumbo look even bigger by comparison, so Barnum presented both elephants alongside one another.

D. HUMBUG! Barnum's "Man-Eating Chicken" was…a *man* who was simply eating chicken!

Picture Credits

Great effort has been made to trace and acknowledge owners of copyrighted materials. Any errors that may have been made are unintentional, and the publisher would be glad to correct them in future printings of this book. The abbreviation "J.G." indicates photos taken by Joshua Gee.

Page 1 © Michael & Patricia Fogden/Minden Pictures.

DRACULA LIVES! 2, left to right: © The Marsden Archive, UK/The Bridgeman Art Library. | © Radu Florescu. 3, left to right: © AFP/ AFP/Getty Images. | © Imagno/Getty Images. 5, left to right: J.G. | © Rosenbach Museum and Library. 6, top to bottom: © Rosenbach Museum and Library. | © Alan Lee. 7: Sam Weber. | 9, top to bottom: © Bettmann/Corbis. | © Ken Schmidt/*Kerville Daily Times*/AP Photo.

IT CAME FROM THE SEA! 10: © Fortean Picture Library | 11: © Mary Evans Picture Library. 12: © The Natural History Museum, London. 13, top to bottom: © HO, National Science Museum/AP Photo. | © Bob Cranston/SeaPics.com. 14, top to bottom: Duncan Wright. | © Norbert Wu (www.norbertwu.com). 15: © Stephen Frink Collection/Alamy. 16: © Courtesy of Ghost Research Society Press. 17: © The British Museum. 18, top to bottom: J.G./The Barnum Museum. | © 2006 Harvard University Peabody Museum, 97-3970/72853 T1383. 19, clockwise: © Courtesy of NOAA Central Library Photo Collection. | © Brandon D. Cole/Bruce Coleman USA (www.bciusa.com). | © Michael Jenner/Alamy.

ALIEN INVASION! 20, top: Private Collection. 21, top: © Bettmann/ Corbis. | Courtesy of UFO Evidence (www.ufoevidence.org). 21, bottom right: © Mark A. Johnson/Corbis. 22, top: John Henshall/Alamy. 23, top: © IKONOS satellite image courtesy of GeoEye. 24, top left to right: © Joe Raedle/Newsmakers/Getty Images. | © 2006 *Roswell Daily Record*. 25, top: © Fortean Picture Library.

HOWLING AT THE MOON! 28: © Polygram/Universal/The Kobal Collection (from *The Howling*). 29, top to bottom: © Polygram/ Universal/The Kobal Collection (from *An American Werewolf in London*). | © Art Resource, NY. 30: © Mary Evans Picture Library/Alamy. 31: © John Kobal Foundation/Getty Images. | Wolf illustrated by Sam Weber. 32: Bone Clones (replica)/J.G. 33, top to bottom: © Sanford/Agliolo/ Corbis. | © Erich Lessing/Art Resource, NY. 35: Shutterstock.

BEWARE OF GHOSTS! 36: Courtesy of Pioneer Press Union City, Tennessee. 37, 38: Robertson County Archives. 39: Shutterstock. 40: Tim Hall/Gregory Rutty. 41: © Fortean Picture Library. 42, left: Kavanagh Family Photo Collection. 42, right, and 43: Dudley Long/ Kavanagh Family Photo Collection. 44: Gregory Rutty.

TO CATCH A GHOST! 46, top to bottom: © Columbia/The Kobal Collection. | © Filmation/Continental Video/Entertainment Rights (UK). 47, top to bottom: © Robertstock/Popperfoto.com. | © Mary Evans Picture Library/Harry Price. 48, all: Paranormal Investigation of NYC. 49–57: All photos taken by J.G.

PHANTOMS ON FILM! 58: © Time & Life Pictures/Getty Images/ Pictures Inc. 60: © National Portrait Gallery, London. 61, left to right: © Thomas Glendenning Hamilton Collection. | © Gérard Lévy Collection, Paris. 62, all: J.G. 63, left to right: © Fortean Picture Library. | J.G. 64, top to bottom: Bassano Ltd./Royal Air Force. | © Mirrorpix. 65, top to bottom: Samantha Schutz. | © Fortean Picture Library.

PERMANENT PETS! 66: John Turnock. 67, top to bottom: Josh Reisner. | © Fortean Picture Library/Alfred Hollidge. 68, clockwise: © Hammer Productions/Everett Collection. | © geogphotos/Alamy. | © Darren Mann. 69, top to bottom: © GK Hart/Vikki Hart/Getty Images. | The Evolution Store/J.G. 70: Shutterstock.

ODD SHOPS & EERIE EATERIES! 72: Grappling hook created by the Mysterious Mister Grutty and photographed by J.G. 73: Scott Irvine (www.scottirvine.net). 74, top: © Courtesy of Garmin Inc. 74, top and bottom, left: Seamus Decker. 74: top and bottom, right: J.G. 75: Tim Hall. 76: Two-headed skeleton created by John Weisgerber. 76 & 77: All photos taken by J.G. and Gregory Rutty. 78, top to bottom: J.G. | Promotional handbill courtesy of Here Arts Center (www.here.org). 79: Puppets created by Erik Sanko (www.eriksanko.com) and photographed by J.G.

AMAZING BRAIN WAVES! 80, top to bottom: © The SORRAT Group/Society for Psychical Research. | © Sven Turck/*Institut fur Grenzgebiete der Psychologie und Psychohygiene, Freiburg im Breisgau*. 81, top to bottom: © 20th Century Fox/Photofest (from *X2: X-Men United*). | Courtesy of the Office of the CIA Information and Privacy Coordinator (Letter to the Author, July 13, 2006). 82: © Michael O'Brien. 83, top to bottom: Courtesy of Paul H. Smith. | © Warner Bros./The Kobal Collection/Jasin Boland (from *The Matrix Reloaded*). 84, left to right: © US Navy/AP Photo. | Courtesy of Paul H. Smith. | 85, top to bottom: US Army/DIA. | CIA. 86: Will Smith/Brian Prothro. 87, top to bottom: © 2006 Sony Computer Entertainment Inc. | "Sonic the Hedgehog" courtesy of Sega Corporation © SEGA. All rights reserved. 88: © Warner Bros./The Kobal Collection (from *The Shining*).

THE BLACK CAT'S PATH! 90: Imagerie D'Epinal. 91, top to bottom: Erik Sanko/Gregory Rutty. | © Chip Somodevilla/Getty Images. | MATCHBOX® is a trademark owned by and used with permission from Mattel, Inc. © 1989 Mattel, Inc. All Rights Reserved. 92 & 93: Tree and gravestone illustrated by Sam Weber. 94: Gregory Rutty. | 95 & 96: J.G. | 97: Gregory Rutty. 98: Tim Hall.

THE FORBIDDEN BOOKSHELF! 100: The Evolution Store/Gregory Rutty. 101 & 102: J.G. 103, clockwise: Benjamin Brown & 31 Down (www.31down.org)/J.G. | © The Trustees of the British Museum | © Courtesy of Tom Sullivan. 104: © *Fate* Magazine Inc.

TO BE OR NOT ZOMBIE! 106 & 107: "Army of Darkness" street performance conceptualized by Jacob Williams (www.jacobwilliamsstudio. com) for the Deitch Art Parade and photographed by J.G. 109: © The Missouri Botanical Garden Library. 110: Victoria Purdie/Bigstockphoto. com. 111, both: © Stephen Frink/Corbis.

TRICKED BY PIXIES! 113: © John Billingsley/Fortean Picture Library. 114 & 115: © Fortean Picture Library. 116, both: © Allistair Mitchell/ Reuters. 117 (magnifying glass): J.G. 117 (mites & "mite poop"): © Microscopix Photo Library.

THE CURSE OF THE MUMMY! 118: © Griffith Institute, 2000–2004. 119: © Paramount Pictures/Photofest. 120 (talisman): J.G. 121: © Smithsonian Institution/Corbis. 122: © Walter Iooss, Jr./*Sports Illustrated*. 123: J.G.

GRUESOME GOOD-BYES! 124, top to bottom: J.G. | © C. Allan Gilbert. 125, top to bottom: © Svensk Filmindustri/The Kobal Collection. | "Death Jr." copyright © 2007 Backbone Entertainment. 127, top: © Glessner House Museum/Courtesy of the Glessner House Museum, Chicago, IL. 127, bottom, 128 & 129: Dollhouse murder scene created and photographed by J.G.

1. **GHOST!** Even before this photo was taken, two-year-old Greg Sheldon Maxwell was fond of pointing into the air and saying, "Old Nanna's here!" His family believed he was referring to his late great-grandmother, who may be posing in the upper left-hand corner of this 1991 snapshot. Nobody else saw anything unusual, and no sources of steam or fog were said to be in the room.

2. **HOAX!** As the hanging lantern and other elements suggest, this is indeed a photo of a woman wearing an old-fashioned black outfit. However, the woman herself is quite alive and doing very well, thank you. She is a costumed tour guide at the Crane-Phillips House in Cranford, New Jersey. Since the house was built in the mid-1800s, electricity wasn't installed until much later. Hence, the "dead" giveaway in this fake ghost photo: Light switches are visible on the wall beside the lantern, revealing that the photo is not as old as it might initially appear. Most experts would be quick to point out another important clue: In the right corner, the bottom of the woman's dress reflects sunlight, creating additional shadows on the bottom left. The first rule of ghost photos is: Ghosts don't have shadows.

3. **GHOST!** His occupation? Airplane mechanic. His name? Freddy Jackson. His time of death? Two days before this photo was taken. Coincidental facelike smudge? You decide. Sir Victor Goddard, retired British Royal Air Force officer, first described this 1919 photo in his memoir, *Flight Towards Reality*. Soon after serving in World War I aboard the HMS *Daedalus*, Freddy Jackson was accidentally killed by an airplane propeller. According to reports, Mr. Jackson's war buddies were quick to identify his likeness in the top row, fourth from the left.

4. **GHOST!** In the front seat of this car is the husband of Mrs. Mabel Chinnery; in the backseat is Mrs. Chinnery's mother…who, by the way, happened to be deceased. Upon inspecting this 1959 photo— taken at the cemetery where Mom was buried— Mrs. Chinnery claimed she instantly recognized the bespectacled form. One photo expert who then analyzed the image reportedly said, "I stake my reputation on the fact that the picture is genuine."

5. **HOAX!** When a camera is set to a low shutter speed, the image will blur if the photographer moves while the shutter is open. Here, a light source in the upper left-hand corner blurred for that reason. It's also worth noting how the *context* of an alleged ghost photo may affect people's interpretations of it. You might have assumed the simplest, least ghostly explanation if the caption hadn't mentioned "an ectoplasmic spiral" and if it hadn't appeared in a chapter called "Phantoms on Film!"

6. **GHOST!** Look at the right side of this image. You might see a girl looking right back at you. Reportedly, Tony O'Rahilly of Wem, England, captured her image on November 19, 1995, as the village's town hall was burning to the ground. The doorway in which she stands was consumed by smoke and flames during the moment when the photo was taken, so no living girl could have been there. According to local legend, O'Rahilly might have photographed a girl who accidentally burned the town to the ground…in 1677.

HOW MANY DID YOU GUESS CORRECTLY?

1–2 out of 6: Perhaps you should take a few night classes…in a haunted house!

3–4 out of 6: You're almost an expert! Next Halloween, be sure to take lots of notes.

5–6 out of 6: Congratulations! You're a true ghost hunter!

Roster

Joshua Gee *Missing since p. 128!*
CHIEF INVESTIGATOR OF THE UNEXPLAINED

Catherine Daly
BOSS OF OFFICIAL OPERATIONS

Tim Hall & Kay Petronio
THE CONSORTIUM OF ADORNERS

**Steven Diamond &
Nicole Durrant**
PURSUERS OF PHOTOGRAPHIC ODDMENTS

Jessica Grindstaff
MOTH WRANGLER

&

The Mysterious Mister Grutty
MISSION SPECIALIST

Special Thanks: Stitch Azintime at Gothic Renaissance | Georgia Barnes | D.R. & S.C. at the Barnum Museum | Kate "Miss Murder" Bell | Shirley & Ben Berzin | The Crane-Phillips House | Brad Davis the Buxtonite | Wade Davis | The Donnelly Family | Kara Edwards | W.S. & A.M. at Evolution | Radu Florescu | Daniel, Joshua, & Thomas Glazer | Michele Higgins | Cynthia & Mark Kavanagh | David Levithan | Abigail McAden | Ministry | Neva & Romeo | The Order of the Teuthida, especially Archie | Paranormal Investigation of NYC | Professor Paranormal | Josh Reisner & Trouble the Cat | Anica Rissi | Y.R. at the Robertson County Archives | M.B., E.F., & G.G. at the Rosenbach Museum & Library | Gregory Rutty | Erik Sanko | Jack & Sally Skellington | Paul & Will Smith | Scott, Seamus, & Fafnir in Surveillance | Tristan, Andy, & Scott in Tactical Ops | J.V., R.H., & 3I Down | Craig Walker | Sam Weber | Jake Williams & his Army of Darkness | M.M. & the Spooky Kids who taught the author how to scream.

There are 101 secrets inside this book.
To discover them all, find EnHo_002 at www.joshuagee.com.

((PAGE 118)) (?)

HALF-BONE, HALF-BANDAGE AND ALL BLOOD-CURDLING HORROR!!

.TO DO.
1) Practice sneer for Photo Shoot.
2) Geocaching ✓
3) Enjoy a delicious feast. ✓
4) Buy bugs. ✓
5) PUPPETS!?!
((PAGE 733))

((PAGE 74?)) #1

DESTINATION: TIMES SQUARE ...or the PARK?

EnHo_001 = E.H.·T.T.!A.V.G.M·M
EnHo_002 = [UPLOAD A.S.A.P.]
EnHo_003 = [??????]
*Conceal on Back CVR

((PAGE 112?))
"FAIRY" or "FAERIE" ✓

"KA..."
S.L...
W...

IMPOSTOR...?

YOU SHAME US!!! CRIME · DO NOT CROSS

WWW.MANORHOUSEMINIATURES.NET

((PAGE 100?))
MEMO to SELF: HAVEN'T SEEN MY EYES FOR DAYS! WHERE ARE THEY???

"TO CATCH A GHOST!"

A GRUESOME GOODBYE
1 inch = 1 foot
FLOOR
HAT
HEADSET
NOT DEAD YET. ONLY A LITTLE!

SPORTS CURSES
OMIT
S.I. Magazine
((PAGE 122?))

FAVORITE 'G' WORDS: GROSS / GRIM / GENUINE / GINORMOUS / GRISLY
GOOSEBUMPS / GORY / GOREY / GROTESQUE / GHOULISH / GHASTLY / GONZO!
GRUESOME

• WWW.FATEMAG.COM
• WWW.CSICOP.ORG/SI
• WWW.NATIONALGEOGRAPHIC.COM

INVENTOR by DAV GHOST HUNTER by NITE ((PAGE 47?))
MODERN MECHANIX AND INVENTIONS
MR. EDISON'S "LIFE UNITS"
(N.Y. TIMES, JAN. 23, 1921)
Hundred Trillion in Human Body May Scatter After Death—Machine to Register Them
MODERN MECHANIX AND INVENTIONS MAGAZINE IS ISSUE 10, Oct. 1933

EXOPOLITICS
= The (theoretical) study of political dealings • between humans and aliens.
VOTE for ME!

((PAGE 74?))
GROUNDWORK? "ALMOST"
#2

((PAGES 62-63?))
PSEUDON
HAT
Doorway
• HAIR
• EYEGLASSES
• NOSE
• MOUTH
• CLOAK
"SIMULACRUM?"

E.H. IMAGE #029
SKULLS
TAKE WOLF SKULL PICTURE ASAP!
BUDGET CODE = OTHER.
FORWARD BILL TO BOSS OF OFFICIAL OPERATIONS

(PREST?)
OMIT for SPACE... NEED PHOTOS BIG!

FAVORITE 'D' WORDS:
1) DREAM
2) DELIRIUM
3) DEATH
4) DESTINY
5) DESTRUCTION.

((PAGE 74?))
BUY WILL AT SHOW?
THE PARK!
#3

PHYSIOLOGY OF THE FEAR RESPONSE
1.) BLOOD PUMPS TO MUSCLES @ 5 TIMES NORMAL RATE.
2.) RAPID INHALATION/EXHALATION, INCREASING FLOW OF OXYGEN TO BLOOD.
3.) BRAIN & PITUITARY GLAND RELEASE ENDORPHINS, WHICH REDUCE SENSITIVITY TO PAIN.
4.) FAT AND GLUCOSE CREATE BURST OF ENERGY.
5.) SWEAT GLANDS HELP PREVENT OVERHEATING.
6.) PUPILS IN THE EYES INCREASE IN SIZE.
7.) THE BODY EXPELS EXCESS WASTE IN ATTEMPT TO STAY LEAN & MEAN.
EXC...

((PAGE 18?))
MAGNETS?

ORIGAMI!
ANCIENT AND FUN ART OF PAPER FOLDING
NOT HORRIFIC
OMIT ALL REFERENCES in text of E.H.!

MEMO to SELF!
LOOK UP.

((PAGE 103?)) (MEANING?)
THE BOOK o' THE DEAD sez:
"I HAVE NOT DRIVEN SMALL CATTLE FROM THEIR HERBAGE." -CH.125
SET

ASTROBIOLOGY
= the study of life in outer space.

((PAGE 49?))
LASER MARKER → Infra Red
INFRA RED THERMOMETER
• ASK THE GHOST HUNTER ABOUT THESE GADGETS!!!

((PAGE 102?)) SPACE 4 CAPTION?
"METRONOMA" WAS CREATED BY 31 DOWN, an NYC THEATER COMPANY BOY. ALL WORK AND NO PLAY MAKES JACK...

CACHE FOUND!
PAGE 74...ay in INCLUDE...arned THE PHOTO...astly!) OF THIS JOURNAL ...ime PAGE? ... Peabo...

ORK AND NO PLAY MAKES DRAC A DULL BOY. ALL WORK AND NO PLAY MAKES DRAC A DULL BOY. ALL WORK AND NO PLAY MAKES DRAC A DULL BOY. ALL WORK AND NO PLAY MAKES DRAC A DULL BOY. ALL WORK AND NO PLAY MAKES DRAC A DULL BOY. ALL WORK AND NO PLAY MAKES DRAC A D...

((PAGE 100?))
A good Book is the precious lifeblood of a master spirit, imbalmed and treasured up on purpose to a life beyond life
-John Milton
$(S=f)$

((PAGE 10?))
NOT HORRIFIC
Zoologists Puzzled Living (Small) Animal Held Extinct 500,000,000 Years
—The New York Times, July 26, 1958
OMIT!